THE LIFELONG MEMORIES OF
JULIE & EDDIE, A LOVE STORY

Edwin P MacNicoll Jr
Author

REVISED EDITION

Edwin P MacNicoll Jr
Copyright@2014

Dedicated to my bride of 53 years

Julianne(Zorichak) MacNicoll

05/20/1940 to 11/30/2011

FOWARD

it is imperative to me that from the beginning, I explain the purpose of this story. It is told at the request of my children and friends. They want me to write my memoirs and our families ancestry which was my mother's last wish. She wanted so badly to discover this, but she never would know since she passed. However it was her desire to be found for her children, her future grandchildren, great grandchildren, and those in the future who might find our life interesting.

The motivation is a combination of a few things. One, I love to remember my past, and two, the absolute truth is that I find that I cannot sleep or stop thinking of my bride and partner, Julie , who is today with God. At their request, I found that I have the time, the ability, and desire to offer my life, since frankly, I find comfort in writing. At this point in my life, it is a form of therapy and pleasure to relive my life. This is not, in any way, a self-serving story. It is a review of the life of two crazy kids that met, fell in love, married, and accomplished a life that we were both proud of.

How does one begin something like this? The truth is that in the world's scheme of things, So, Julie and our life are and were really nothing. Yet we lived and we shared things many people never utterly understood.

It has always been my belief, and I will repeat this over and over again in the body of this book, that Julie and I both adored words and their meaning. God gave us, among other things, two gifts that so many folks appreciate or realize.

They are Love and Memories.

I hope, in my humble endeavor, to demonstrate the meaning of them both as I see them in my words. I would like you to always remember after reading my story that both love and memories are God's never-ending gifts. Memories is a blessing since we remember at times we need to, our youth, our growing up, and all those previous lessons we learned from our parents. Our neighbors,

Our teachers and friends combined make us who we are today.

Love:

 Love really needs no explaining from me at all, you simply understand it, or you don't. Love is with each of us from the day we are born and follows us to our last days. God alone gives us all unconditional and continuous love. Each person in his or her lifetime will hear and also say the words "I love you" thousands and thousands of times. From loved ones, on the TV, movies, radio, or read these words. You have to know the meaning of this word, Love.

 Memories:

These are the never-ending gifts that give us the ability to recall all things, both good and bad, that have happened in our lives. It allows you to return repeatedly to your past, to take you back in time and to remember your loved ones, to allow you to remember incredibly special and precious events in your life that you share with no one. Memories also allow you to see the faces of those so dear to you. There is absolutely no end to what your memory can offer you. These memories, like love, are with you until your last days.

Both are free:

This book therefore is my memoirs of love. As I look back and recall my life, I hope to show you a true love story of my family and my love story of my bride Julie.

My story will be about a family and personal history. It is about a family moving to Trenton, NJ. Growing up during the wonderful war years and how it really was during that time.

Stories of the folks that lived on the street, the lessons learned, how the neighbors all banded together, and other true stories of that period. Stories of the hardships of that time. A tribute to all the similar northeastern communities and towns lining Trenton, NJ. All showed the act of working together and putting up a patriotic front that was never known to man before. Also meeting many celebrities along the way.

A story of a boy that went from not being able to read or write to a husband , father, and grandfather; realtor; a national instructor; national public relations chairman; an author; an instructor's instructor to the National Presidency of one of America's largest appraisal organizations.

I might not be able to say, tell, or express the love we shared. I don't ever

Comment [EM]:

image there is no viable way that you can understand the love I had for my bride.

I intend to remember and write all I can. I will start with my mother and father's lives as was told to me. Of how they came to Trenton. Then I will reveal how it was during those times, a story of someone who was there, and lived during the Depression and World War II era.

It seems that somehow, I was blessed and given the talent to be able to remember my past. In fact, I can see things as they were. God has always given me the love for words even though I quit school in the seventh grade and could not really read or spell when Julie and I married.

Though this story will include Julie, I cannot document her early childhood, other than what she had told me. Although she was four years younger that I, she lived and faced many similar experiences that I did. She was born on May 25, 1940, to Urban and Mary Zorichak. At that time, she had an older brother Urban Jr. and an older sister Patricia. She would later have a younger brother Albert.

Her father worked as a laborer for the Pennsylvania Railroad. Her mother was sickly most of Julie's life with periods of depression and Parkinson disease. This caused Julie and her brothers and sisters to at times be separated within the family group. As a girl, Julie mostly lived with her grandparents.

I discovered that she too was once in the same orphanage that I was sent to, that I will write about in this story. Julie's relatives were loving, caring, and giving people, including her aunt, her mother's sister, a catholic nun, who was a mother's superior. Her name was Sister Marie Pauline.

After Julie's mother sickness became stabled, Julie's life was normal, and she attended catholic schools most of her life. She was a very devoted, religious girl and she graduated in 1958 from Saint Mary's Cathedral, which was the church in which we were married.

I hope my story to my family, relatives, and friends who might be interested, will show that dreams can come true and that with the help of God and a loving spouse you can achieve and live a fruitful, productive, and wonderful life.

Julie and I were not special people in any way. We were just the typical husband and wife, son, daughter, mother, and father like zillions of folks before us.

It is important to me that you note that in this story, you will not find anything that is not the truth. In thinking and contemplating just how to write this, I decided that I will simply write it as I remember it from the time, I was a child.

Coming to Trenton

But I will begin the story of my mother and father, their early lives, how they met, and just how our family started. This is all from research and my memory, with a good portion of what my mother and father have told me over the years.

At this point, I must tell you about both my mother and father. My dad was born in Philadelphia in 1907. His father, Alexander, was killed in the 1917 explosion at the Eddystone Arsenal. After his father died, my father was placed at an orphanage for twelve years. My mother was born in Norristown, PA, and her mother died at age thirty-seven. Then Mom grew up with a relative that didn't want or love her.

They both grew up in a lonely, loveless atmosphere. These were two extremely wonderful people who suffered a tragic eruption in their young lives which was caused by the sudden early deaths of my father's father and my mother's mother.

As a result, their brothers and sisters were forever separated and were scattered to the winds. Never knowing where each were. You will read later that Julie and I found a few after sixty years.

Because of their loss of family, neither ever had a real Christmas, birthday parties, or spent Easter as a loving family just as institutionalized children. Therefore, they never really had a real sense of love, or what a stable family life was like. However, both wanted children and a family badly.

Somehow, they both found each other while working and living on the grounds at Norristown State Hospital. They fell in love and married. In sharing their pasts, mom told me that they both promised each other to always remain together and to try to have children.

And to always make sure that they were taken care of, loved, and given things that they never had.

After their marriage, they had a baby girl, Thelma MacNicoll, that died a few days after birth. Mom was devastated and sad and because of the rules of the hospital since mom had given birth and because of this they both a something they had anticipated and only lost places they could go, was my mother to share a room with a friend in a house nearby and my dad could go back with his family.

This was in a time in America when employment was scarce and families where living two or more families in a home to share expenses. The Depression was cruel and heartbreaking on many families, very few people had steady or full-time jobs then and the chances of finding employment was not good.

My father's mother had remarried and had no room for my mom. So they were separated Facing the fact that they now had no place to live, no jobs, and no future, they did not like the separation and wanted to stay together and do something.

The following is what my mother told me.

Dad remembered that he had a friend that lived in Trenton, NJ, who offered to let them stay and find work. So, with only a few dollars and their belongings, they left his mother's home in the rain.

It was raining and they walked across Ben Franklin Bridge and found shelter in an old, abandoned house at the foot of the bridge. They spent the night there. They were carrying all the belongings they had.

The next morning, they started to hitchhike on the highway to Trenton. Mom said that a large "touring-type car" stopped with a man driving. He asked where they were going, and he told them that was where he was headed. As they drove, Mom found out his name. She said she didn't want to , but she cried when she explained to him that they had lost both their employment at the hospital and the death of their daughter.

Mom said that in that single moment God looked down on them. They discovered that this man was a high official at the Trenton State Hospital and that was where he was going.

Noting their sorrow and need, and the fact that they both had experience in hospitals, he told them that he might be a help, but he knew he could get at least one of them a job there right away. He felt also that he that he could offer them a place to stay on the grounds as well. Mother became a nurse . My parents were forever indebted to this man who became a friend. Mom said that God sent him to them, and we believed that to be so. Mom and Dad worked and lived in hospital-provided sleeping quarters until my sister Joyce was born.

The hospital rules did not allow children to live there so they moved to Washington Crossing, NJ (right where General George Washington crossed the Delaware that night in 1776.). Dad still worked there, and Mom continued to work off-and-on part time. I was born on leap day, February 29, 1936, I(Leap Years day) In Mercer Hospital in Trenton, NJ. However, I lived in Washington Crossing, NJ., My father did get his job back temporarily.

Things were still very unstable and bad at this time . The Great Depression had continued to cause many families to break up and the tough times caused folks to share and again live-in overcrowded houses and apartments.

For a while mom and dad were lucky because my dad worked at the hospital and for the bar general store across the road, known at that time as the "Tally Ho."

But then things turned bad. Dad got laid off from the hospital , and since he did not make enough money at the general store, we could not afford to live here, and we had to move to a place with lower rent. We moved house in Trenton. (The house is no longer there). It was behind Van Skiver's Furniture Store. It was at this time my brother Henry was born. We were living as all families were at that time, from paycheck to paycheck.

 For some unknown reason, my father one day abandoned us and went to his family in Philadelphia. Dad left without saying anything to my mom and she had only a few dollars and little food in the house. Henry was a baby, and he was extremely sick.

Mom was crushed and did not know what to do. She never expected this and was devastated. It was winter and she was alone with four children and no money for coal to heat or food. For the very first time faced with this, Mom said that she did not know what to do. Up until this time, she knew that times had been hard, but she felt that they were in love, and they had the family they dreamed of for so long, and up until now, they faced each bump in the road that they encountered together.

She was extremely hurt, surprised, and totally confused. No, she could not believe what was happening. All she could think of was that her children might take away as it was with her family Because of her childhood and being very unfamiliar with the laws of New Jersey, my mother feared that the authorities could take her children and she would never let that happen, so decided right then that she had to be strong and protect us children.

Mom told me that she knew at that especially important moment, that she would never, ever let anything happen to us kids like it happened to her and her family.

She talked to the landlord, who did not care. So, at the end of the month, we were thrown out of the house. Mom said she pleaded. But they didn't care; it was cold and snowing as she sat on the porch with us crying. All our belongings were on the curb with Joyce, Ethel, me, and Henry who was extremely sick at this time and running a high fever.

She was helpless, scared and did not know what to do or what was going to happen to us. A neighbor called the church, and they took us all to the Salvation Army Building, then to Brunswick , and took Henry to the hospital and took us out of the snow and the cold.

Mom said that she was incredibly grateful that we were out of the weather, safe for now, but had an uneasy fear. She knew that she had to go to the hospital with Henry, who was then hospitalized for a few days, but she was so, so afraid that the authorities might take us away from her for being penniless and homeless at the time. She did not know the laws and did not trust anyone at the time.

We would spend the next nine months safe, warm, and well fed, living in the basement of the Salvation Army with all the other folks there.

My father, reconsidering, found out where we were, and he returned. He and mom talked and worked things out. He had inherited money and just stayed away , but he discovered that he loved my mom and us kids and returned. He was deeply sorry and of course mom forgave him , because she loved him so.

None of us will really ever know about our dad's actions, but at this point in this story, I must stop and point out that during this extremely hard period in America, many fathers, overcome with the responsibility of a family, just left them and moved on. This selfish and cowardly act was widespread. In defense of my father, my mother told me years after that my father was a really a good man who made a mistake and unlike those cowar4ds,l he returned and was always faithful and honest with her. He remained with us all his life and raised nine children. Dad loved us all.

At this time, despite the conditions, mom so desperately wanted us to all live in a house and not once more and be a family. My dad then got a good steady job and the authorities helped us find a new home. However, even with my dad's job , things were still bad and our family, like many families, still needed help with food, medical care, and clothing. Then World War II started.

We moved for three different and then finally to a section known as

Chambersburg in about 1941
We stayed there until 1948. All of these moves were taken because we were all on some type of welfare as most families were at that time
Our family was helped by catholic groups, one being the Mount Carmel Guild.

 Dad was then called to the army and was sent to Lake Charles, Louisiana.

 The street we lived on, Locust Street, is a place I will never forget. On one side of the street there was a row of brick homes, all with porches, or stumps as we called them, and on our side of the street there were semidetached homes with portico porches.

I was about five years old at this time. At the time, the war was on and most of the able men were gone, they enlisted or were drafted. There were kids all up and down the street of all nationalities. Also, at that time there were many families living here that were known as

"DPs " (displaced persons) that had fled Hitler from all different counties.

It was so pleasant and nice. Each day we would have vendors come up the street. At that time, men made deliveries to your door. Ice Man, Bread Man, Milk Man, and produce men who came with a horse and wagon.

Also, during World War II, doctors came to your home when you were sick. If someone were really sick, they would put a quarantine sign on your door. No one could go in or out.

I remember those days with a smile , because your family might have been quarantined, but your neighbors knew it and these caring folks, knowing we had kids, would spend the day cooking their favorite dish and came to our side window.

"Here Mrs. MacNicoll, I cooked this for your family. Enjoy." Wow! Who would do this today???

My Mom did the same thing for other families many, many times. You must remember there was at this time five children in my family . Like us, these folks had few things to give, but caring, prayers, food, and love.

Everything was rationed in those days. A ration coupon book was issued to every person living in the United States of America during this time, even newborn babies. Since most everything was going to the war effort, everyone had to share the sacrifice.

I LOVE REMEMBERING THIS, BECAUSE IT WAS HOW I GOT TO ENJOY ETHNIC FOODS.

WINDOW STAR FLAGS:

In most of the windows all over America the folks that had loved one in the place where folks service proudly hung a service flag—known as Stars. A blue star meant that a loved one was serving overseas. A silver star meant that a loved one was wounded, and a gold star meant that a loved one was killed in action. The army and navy used to arrive with the sad news, or they used telegrams. I remember a few times the silence of a summer's day was broken by the scream and cries of a mother or wife just receiving news that they lost a loved one. One can never forget such a thing. All the women on the block would rush to console her. It was sad, but it happened many, many times.

The women on the block were mothers, sisters, girls , and single women . I remember how they all got together on someone's front porch and talked about living together and how they could help each other in times of crisis and how to take care and watch over all of the kids.

The women knew two things, we were hungry a lot and that we grew out of our clothes. They shared food and each offered hand-me-downs to whoever could use them.

On our street there were two older ladies that had been extraordinarily rich but lost everything in the crash of the Depression. These were very educated women that offered their advice and acted almost as our street's lawyers. Those wonderful, patriotic women helped us all make life a little better.

These women took care of each other and all the kids on the block. During this stressful time, the other kids and I were also taught a lot of valuable lessons of life. We learned these things, not only from Momma and Dad, but from the women of the street, the local policemen, next-door neighbors, teachers, nuns, and the people at the corner store. One lesson was respect, sharing and helping each other anyway we could. As kids, we were all taught to respect our elders, other people, other folk's property, and their feelings. As I sit here today, my mind races back and I remember the many lessons I was taught about respect.

The women uin the country also had to help out and went to work in factories. They were busy making battleships, cruisers, tanks, airplanes, guns and everything for the war effort, there was an immediate for manufacturing jobs for all those who could work, and the women became mothers and factory workers at the same time. During this era.

At this point I would like to tell you a simple story of just one of the many lessons I learned.

Mom loved people and tried to help everyone, just as many other mothers did. During the war, my mom always really worried about the older neighbors, especially when it snowed.

She would get us kids to go up and down our block sweeping off the porches and steps and throwing ashes on the sidewalks so they would not slip.

Across from us there lived an Italian man named Tony and his wife. I never knew her real name, he just called her Momma. Tony was about sixty at the time, about five-foot-four-inches and about 110 pounds. His hair was still black with traces of gray. His skin showed the tan he had from working in his yard. His hands and his fingers were bent and twisted from something . Both his hands and face were wrinkled, and he always spoke in that wonderful Italian broken English.

One winter day I had cleaned off his porch and was putting ashes on his sidewalk, Tony opened the door. He smiled and waved his wrinkled fingers at me to come to the door, which I did. He then tried to hand me a nickel. This was the very first time I was close to him.

"No," I said. "But thank you ." I turned and walked over the snow to my house across the street. I need to tell you, I was not happy with myself—God , which was five cents. I really wanted it too. But momma told us never, ever to take money. We did this simply as good neighbors. With those five cents I could have bought five grab bags at the store. Now for you younger folks, in those years, merchants took three or four pieces of candy, put them in small bags, then put them in a big box and sold them for a penny a bag. You just reached in and took one. We called them grab bags.

I saw Tony again sometime in the spring, he came over to ask mom if he could use me to help him. Of course, Mom said yes. I entered Tony's house and he shouted, "Momma, give this boy a drink," and she did. Tony and Momma had two gold stars in both front windows. I knew what these gold star banners meant they had lost a son or a daughter in the war. They had two hanging in each window . I would find out later that they had two sons, Nicky was a sailor killed in the pacific and Tony Jr. was killed, of all places, Italy. --- Even thought I was young, I understood their great loss, but all I could do was marvel. They were both extraordinarily strong folks to bear that every day.

Their house was a small row home with two bedrooms, there were once three but when indoor plumbing came in, they filled up the old out house and made the rear bedroom a bath. Tony's yard was important to him. In the summer he took everyone there. He had an overhead, grape-growing trestle and it was shady and cool under there. I would get to spend many, many days with my new friend. Tony also had a chicken coup at the end of the yard. He once told me he put the coup over the old out house. He thought the chickens gave better eggs because of that. That still makes me laugh. So, he took me to the backyard and said to me in broken English, "You know my name" to which I said no.

"It is Mr. Tony Z. But you are my friend; you call me Tony...OK?"

I smiled and said, "Sure Tony."

Then he said, "Momma and I will call you Eddie—OK Momma?"

"Sure," she said as she came out the door with   iced tea. Momma was forever offering me food. That's how I officially became their friend.

Now for the lesson I got from this--- Tony, like a lot of folks, made their wine. Sometimes he drank too much. It was a real sweltering day when Tony spotted me sitting on my porch and waved me over.

"Eddie, I got a lot of corn and spring beans I want you to help me with." He would always give me enough of anything he had to take home for my family. So, we sat in the backyard under the shade of the grapes, and we were shucking corn and spring beans, he had bushels of them. I could see that Tony had been "Tasting his wine."

 He had that Italian stogie in the left side of his mouth and was sweating a bit. Tony loves to wear Lee Overalls Bib pants and today he had one on, but no shirt. As we worked, he said he had his friends over and told them to leave because they were talking about his neighbors.

He looked at me as I was working and said. *"You know Eddie, some peoples is crazy. They just hate and they hate, Tony does not understand. If you have a fight and no longer like an Italian guy or a polish guy and Irish, then you are mad with them, not the family or all Italians, Polish, or Irish, right? These folks because they are mad, hate their families their moms and dads, their friends, their cats and dogs, everything."*

Then there was a long silence, he turned his head and looked at me through his glasses with his left eye closed and the right open. He smiled and said, *"You know Eddie, I think the also hate their chickens."*

At that time, many neighbors had chicken coups in their yard. That made me laugh.

After we were done, he took my hand in his and looked me in the eyes and said, *"Eddie, I know you and I know your momma and poppa. You are good folks. Tony wants you to promise me as you grow up to be a man. You will never be like those haters."* He rubbed his hand through my hair, pulled he to his chest to hold me, and said as he laughed,

"Remember, just because you donna like one chicken, don't mean all the chickens are bad."

A silly lesson, huh . I get tears in my eyes as I remember his words to me. He was a man that old Ed will never forget. But these trivial things given and learned as children, one at a time, then combined into many are the things we all were taught by not only our loved ones, but others . I love remembering, it brings me joy. I am a son of the city of Trenton and all those great moms and dads, all those wonderful neighbors and folks that made me what I am today. · Dad was raised catholic since he was in an institution. Mom was raised with really no religion. However, they had all of us children raised as catholic.

We all went to the catholic school.

During that troubled time in our world history when Dad, like others, were away in the war, there was a crucifix of Jesus on the cross on our dining room wall. In many ways, it was the center of our world during those time since it received many prayers from us kids on our knees. Though it was true that we learn about God in school, Mom and Dad taught us about God long before our first school day.

EXPERIMENTAL DRUG:

I remember that I had a serious ear infection, and my ear would drain and hurt. Mom took me one day in front of the crucifix and called my brothers and sisters and we got on our knees. Mom said, "We must pray to God. Your dad is not here, and Eddie needs to get to the hospital. They want to use a new drug on him. It is what they call an experimental drug." We prayed and I was taken to Saint Francis Hospital where they stuck me with a needle every four hours. I was one of the many human volunteers for this wonderful, life-saving drug.

It worked. The name of that new drug was Penicillin. They then rushed to the war front lines to give to the troops.

THE STREET:

This next part might be hard for some to believe, but it was true all over the county at this time. No one had money, so when someone died, the practice was to have the funeral in the house. The front of the home or living room was mostly used. The local funeral director would take out the windows or doors to get the casket in and out. The funeral director always used folding chairs. After the service, they were placed in the dining room for visitors and family. The kitchen and the backyard is where the adults went to talk, smoke, or drink.

I smile as I remember that these precious times, the church, and the streets were full of women who all wore black to respect the family. Neighbors would offer and prepare the refreshments for the family; many times, they took the family's children for a few days to give the adults some grieving time. The priests and nuns were available and helpful. I witnessed, as a child, a few very emotional caskets serviced from our front porch.

I remember all these things. The people of my street, they all, over the years, became part of me and who I became. The lessons I learned during that time had latched themselves on to my mind and my heart.

THE BETRAYAL:

I remember one long, sizzling summer, his sister Trudy was expected to be born. One of the ladies from the Mount Caramel guild talked my mother into allowing them to take Ethel, Myself, Henry, Anthony, and Billy to a "farm" for a few weeks in order to give mom a little rest. It was described as just a farm with cows, chickens, and ducks. It would only be for a few weeks.

However, we soon find out that it was a catholic orphanage. There were hundreds of children here. The nuns were extremely strict and used harsh treatment with us. It was not what we thought, and we were terribly upset. I proved to be the troublemaker, insisting we be allowed to go back home. I was beaten with an ironing cord, twice. My back was on fire.

It was a Sunday, I was about seven then, we were to go to church, but I wanted to escape so I climbed out a second-story window, fell to the ground, not hurting myself, and ran down a country road. I have no idea where I was or where I was going. Soon as I was walking, I saw a farmer walking out to his mailbox. He stopped me and asked where I was going. I lied and told him that I got off the wrong stop on a bus and was trying to get home. I didn't know if he believed me, but he took me inside his kitchen where his wife and mother were. They fed me oatmeal and said that they were on their way to church in Trenton. They asked me my address which I had memorized.

Then we drove in his jeep. I was in the back with his mother, and they drove me to my house. Mom was outside talking to a neighbor when we arrived and was shocked to see me. I told her about the farm, which was not a farm but an orphanage, then I showed her my back. Mom went crazy. She thanked the farmer over and over again for getting me home safely and she ran to the store on the corner to call the lady. There were only a few telephones at that time in our area. Mom was so mad.

"They lied to me," she said . "Just like they lied to my family when they took my brothers and sisters away." Within four or five hours a car with Ethel, Henry, Anthony, and Billy pulled up and they were home also.

That is when mom told me that as a child, right after her mother died, a nice lady came and talked to her and her family. The nice lady told them all that they were all going to be taken to farms where the farmer's and wives wanted to have children and that they would be well taken care of and loved. Mom said that was all a lie. She found out that these farmers just wanted children for cheap labor. They gave them room and board but treated them badly. I remember her words and the look on her face, since at this time she had no idea where her sisters and brothers where, or even if they were still alive.

A few days later my sister Trudy was born. They put a bed in the dining room, and she was born in the house. The two mothers that helped the doctor where next door neighbors on both sides, Girdy Fink and Rosie Letho. Mom named her Gertrude Rose MacNicoll after them.

Yes, being raised in the 1930s and 1940s , which were hard and difficult on all people worldwide. The world during those years is so different that today. A completely different world. Here is another thing I remember and want to share:

During the war, all over the country, folks were encouraged to grow their own food. They were known as "Victory Gardens."

The folks on my block really got into this and brought all us kids into it too. It was exciting to grow vegetables of our own, just from seeds. All kinds of seeds were given free and almost everyone grew in their backyard or on vacant lot all kinds of vegetables for their families. In the fall we all would get together and harvest, then prepare these foods for the winter months. I helped in picking the vegetables, washing out the mason jars, filling the jars, using hot wax to seal them, and then placing them in storage for winter.

In addition, there were a few different produce men who used to travel up and down the streets (with a horse and wagon) to make sure that housewives had fresh bananas and vegetables. Even though most households had backyard gardens, grapes, bananas, and other stuff they didn't grow made the produce men's rounds profitable. I remember that all foods like potatoes, tomatoes, spring beans, corn, apples, and others where in hundred-pound bags or bushel baskets.

One produce man had a horse that used to know the route better than he did. And right after the war, he had a truck.

He kept his rounds right up to when we moved. It gave people a chance to catch up on the news while getting really fresh items for the table. If people did have a car, it would be used for work. Women had to walk long distances to get to our tiny grocery and children made it too difficult to go often. The produce man was an immense help.

During those years, all the women on your street acted like they were your mother. There were three regular policemen that walked the beat. They knew your names and we all knew theirs.

One of the best things was the movies. We had a few movie theaters in our area. The Gaiety Theater on Olden Avenue, the Greenwood Theater on Greenwood Avenue, and the Park Theater. For a few cents you could see a news reel, a comic, and two full-featured movies. If you came in late, you could sit and watch it over and over again. Of course, there was no air-conditioning at all until after the war.

Then on Saturday night when mom could afford it, she would walk to the drug store and buy funny books , known today as comic books.

We kids were always trying to make money. Milk and soda bottles at that time had a deposit. Two cents for soda bottles and five cents for milk or large soda bottles. We hunted everywhere for them. We shoveled snow, carried packages from the markets, cleaned out garages and attics, and whatever someone was willing to give us a little money for.

THE SUMMER DAYS:SCHOOL WAS OUT!

I remember when vacation time came. School is over. Mercer County schools were closed until September.

I remember getting up, seeing the sunshine, and wondering what to do first. Going out on the porch, looking up and down the street, looking for other kids that might be up now.

Smiling and happy as I got dressed in my jeans and sneakers. Eating breakfast, promising Mom that I would be good and that I won't go too far away.

Remembering that very first step off my porch and the feeling of freedom. Thinking of what to do first. Go to the playground, go to my best friend's house, and get him.

Then I saw a few kids on the swings at the playground and I ran to get a swing, but I had to wait.

"Come on guys, let me swing," I moaned until they let me. I swing and pull myself high, then higher, and higher. I could feel the wind and sun on my face. I push harder and I am at this minute so happy, my mind cannot stop thinking of what I wanted and hoped to do this summer vacation.

Soon the new playground instructor arrives. She is beautiful: red hair, green eyes, and green shorts. All the boys in the playground are instantly drawn to her and gather around the picnic table, which will be her headquarters from now on. I am not sure, but I am in love. Yes, that fast! Naw, but she sure is cute. She takes time to introduce herself and sets up her table. Suddenly I noticed that there are no girls here yet. I soon will find that it seems to always take a while for the girls to arrive. Hmmm.

I play her games, listen to her instructions, hear her stories, and then go back to playing with the guys. We didn't have real baseball equipment. Instead we had a brick wall on the side of the house. We drew a big stick-zone box on the wall; found an old broom strike handle and an old tennis ball; and we played "Stick Ball ." Let me tell you, this game had to be invented by God, it so good. We played the day away.

 Before lunch, it clouds up and we have a soft summer shower. I stand in the rain, but then I rush to a friend screened porch with many other kids and I wait a short while until it stops. At various times we stop playing to go home for lunch or to go to the puttie.

After lunch, the sky is sunny once again and it gets hot. I lay on the grass on my back looking up at the blue sky and the moving clouds. I spread my legs and my arms. This is a great first day of summer.

We play; get to know each other better that day. Go home for dinner and we play out on the porch in the evening, with Mom and Dad on the porch talking to neighbors. It was then we were all taught once again the "Street Light Rule." You must be home when the streetlights come on. Then it's in the house, on the floor around the big radio, and listening to the shows.

Then upstairs to bed. I smile and I am happy, knowing this all starts over again tomorrow.

MY BUS ADVENTURES:

Mom and Dad did not drive. We had no money and you needed gas stamps.

After the war ended in the 1940s, the manufacturing in Trenton went crazy. Folks had jobs. There was a sense that the future for all of us was particularly good. For so many years folks had sacrificed. With a feeling of pride, they now filled the jobs that were available. The factories were suddenly always working twenty-four hours a day. Known then as "Shift Work."

You actually could quit one job and go across the road and get hired. There was

General Motors, General Electric, De Laval, Lee Overalls, Dermoid, American Pottery, Trenton Potties, potty and rubber factories, Horsemen Dolls, CV Hill, Circle F, and John A Roebling and Son's US Steel Works.

The folks were happy; it was the beginning of a new and exciting era. They had put off buying new things for years and every day there seemed to be a new and exciting product placed on the market. There were no suburban shopping centers as there are today, there were only the Mom-and-Pop shops and stores in Trenton.

My best friend at that time, Ronnie, and I loved going exploring. We were old enough and we made our own money by cutting grass, carrying packages, and filling shelves for the neighborhood store.

At that time, the city was serviced by the Trenton Transit Bus Company, whose big garage was on East State

Street near Olden Avenue. I tell you that in those days, everybody and I mean everybody took the bus, at least twice a day, going and coming from work. There were bus routes all over Trenton, Hamilton, Ewing, Princeton, Pennington, Lawrence, and East Windsor. The buses ran from about six a.m. to eight p.m. every fifteen or twenty minutes.

They came out with something called a "Bus Pass." It cost so much a week, but it was very reasonable for everyone to afford. This pass could be used by anyone in the family without a ride limit.

Ronnie and I saved our money, and, with our parent's permission, we started to have adventures. We would take rides on each route. We would ride them all the way to the end and return home. We tried them all, it was fun. There was no air conditioning, so the windows were always open and down. Ronnie and I traveled these routes many times, we used our family Bus Pass, and it did not cost us a cent. We were on a great, new adventure. I remember all the folks we met and made friends with during our travels.

The bus drivers were great people. Men back from the war, happy to have a job, and caring for their loved ones. One driver told me he didn't care what anyone thought that he was glad to be a bus driver, and his wish was to be the best bus driver there was. That was the way many men felt at that time. Not caring about the type of job, but the wish to be the best they could.

Anyway, Ronnie and I would save our money and on Fridays we would go to Downtown Trenton. We caught the bus on Hamilton Avenue and soon we would be at State and Broad Street. The center of Trenton. There were many buses lined up picking up passengers. They were all going in all kinds of directions on different routes.

You younger folks might not believe this, but in those days the streets downtown every day, even the weekends, were filled with people. Like us, most people were there to spend the day window shopping. In the fall around Halloween, stores had contests and awarded great prizes for the student who could paint the best picture on their store windows. We loved to just see their paintings and see the names of the student artists.

It was so busy on the sidewalks you sometimes had to walk in the street. On Broad Street in front of Yards Department Store, there was a little shack-like stand that was the Bus Dispatcher. He was there all-day answering questions for folks on how to get various places and to route the buses.

You could smell Planters Peanuts as soon as the bus doors opened. Cars were riding up and down the street and the traffic cop wore a white cap. Folks were crossing the street.

Ronnie and I loved the five and ten cents stores on East State Street and visited all of them. It smelled so good in those stores. We might visit the famous lunch counters and would go out the side door to Broad Street. I loved to walk down South Broad Street to the Sun Ray Drug Stores across from Sam Stern's Department Store, then walk back up to see what movies were coming to the Capitol Theater. Maybe buy a comic book at the paper stand at State and Broad Street or go to Nedrick's for a hot dog and orange drink. Then we walked up State Street to Warren Street to see what movies were coming to the Trent Theater or to the Lincoln Theater. Sometimes we might go into Texas Wieners or the Chinese restaurant on the corner, or the Ice Cream shop across the street where all the girls from Saint Mary's Cathedral went all the time.

I was totally in love with the Stacy Trenton Hotel and Hotel Hilde Brecht. I loved to see the lobby and see the folks going in and out. They were the closest thing I knew of as a palace at that time. Both grand hotels, they were the pride of Trenton. The splendor of their architecture was overwhelming to me.

Usually from there we would travel home. This is a small part of the many adventures Ronnie, and I took in our adventures of the city we loved and grew up in.

OUR EASTERS:

Please note that none of these stories are meant in any way to enlist sympathy on us poor kids at that time. At that time, we didn't know any other way. We didn't know we were poor. And you must remember that everything being made, grown, or manufactured then was going to the war effort exclusively. Yes, it is true we didn't have much.

We would get new clothes twice a year for the first day of school and at Easter. Easter was a dress-up day for most of us. In those days, Easter meant going to church. The men always wore hats and women, and girls had the traditional Easter Bonnets.

I would like to point out that even though there was a war going on and loved ones were away, Moms were here at home with us kids and time after time with no money used all their knowledge, skills, and resources in providing for their kids.

I am going to take you back to one on my Easters. There were no Easter baskets unless you had one in the attic. So, my mother and the other mothers did something else. They made their own. Beautiful, homemade Easter baskets.

Mom used a good, old All fathers Easter egg box, which held the yellow center coconut cream Easter eggs. She cut off the top of the box and cut it in two to make the handles. She used a few fly clips to hold them on. Then she used different Easter color crepe paper and wrapped the box. She finished them with assorted color ribbons, using the blade of the knife to curl them. I remember so well what beautiful colors they were. For grass, Mom cut up plain wax paper and put it in the bottom of the basket.

Then she placed that wonderful All fathers egg in the middle, the colored eggs we all colored, and jellybeans.

No one in my neighborhood had an Easter basket and this Easter Recital felt like it went on for years. You could not find your basket until after church and of course after you took your good clothes off.

My mom made sure Easter was great.

MEETING A FUTURE CELEBRITY:

This is a true story . It's about a man who would years later become famous and a movie and Television icon. But at the time neither he nor any of us knew he would be. He went on to be a great and loved comedian and movie star. He was a funny man from my past.

I think, but I am not sure, it was 1946. I had a good friend. His name was Ronnie. I am not sure about all the dates I am going to talk about. But I hope your find this little story interesting.

Ronnie and I had another friend that lived on Tyler Street near Chambers, so we were always near Trenton High School.

If you can picture Trenton High School, where the front circular drive is . This funny man at times would park on

Chambers in right-about the middle of the circle.

Ronnie and I looked for him all the time. He was funny, a good guy, and the back of his car yielded riches to us many times in the form of soda bottles, which we would deposit for the refund. .

This guy loved RC Cola, or Royal Crown Cola for you younger folks. He also loved devil dog's cakes. The back of his car was a pig pen. He read a lot of newspapers, drank a lot of sodas, and ate many types of cakes. When finished, he threw the wrappers over his shoulder to the back seat.

Ronnie and I first discovered them one day after walking up and seeing a bottle laying on the back seat. We stopped and asked if we could have it.

He said, "Look, it's the dead-end kids." He called Ronnie "Jr " after that and I was just the kid, since I was younger than Ronnie. We laughed at him and were told, "Go away kids," but we wanted that two-deposit bad. So, we begged. Finally, he said, "Tell you what, see all that junk in the back, papers and things? If you guys fold those papers and put the wrappers in that bag, you can have all the bottles in there." "Sure," we said, and Ronnie and I started our work. It was a bonanza for us; we found seven bottles, wow! Fourteen cents. We were rich. We did our job, took the garbage, and placed it on the curb across the street, since the garbage men were not there yet.

We then looked for him all the time around the neighborhood and found him a lot. Sometimes we got four bottles, sometimes two. I asked him his name and he kidded us and said, "My name is Charlie."

We lost track of him, until a few months later. Ronnie and I belonged to troop #35, which met in the gym at Saint Mary's Cathedral. We had to take the bus to town, and we saw him again on the corner of State and Warren Streets. He was standing in front of the cigar store talking to some men. That's when we found out his real name was Ernie Kovacs. Our scout master knew him and told us that he wrote a column for the Trentonian. That explained all those newspaper in his back seat. Then Ronnie and I found out that he had a radio show also. It was with WTTM, which at that time was located on E State Street on the block between the YMAC and Lee Overalls. We went to see him.

Then Ernie went on to have a TV morning show out of Philadelphia. You need to know that at this time, TV did not have twenty-four-hour schedules. At night, after the Late, Late Show they would go off the air and return in the morning. Ernie's show was called Three to Get Ready . it was from Monday through Friday between seven to nine in the morning. He was so, so, so funny.

Mom had to push me out of the door to go to school.

The last time I saw Ernie was at the entrance of Saint Francis Hospital. He was with some Trenton friends, and I saw the beautiful Edie Adams for the first and last time. Ernie went to Hollywood, and she too became a famous movie and television star

Ronnie and I did not know at the time that we were given the used bottles of a future movie star. They were given to two kids he would never remember now that he was a famous personality and groundbreaker in the movie and entertainment business.

For those that might not know, this famous son of Trenton, when he died, his pallbearers were some of the most popular movie stars and famous singers of all time, these were his friends.

Jack Lemmon, Frank Sinatra, Dean Martin, Billy Wilder, and George Burns,

Groucho Marx, Edward G. Robinson, Kirk Douglas, Jack Benny, James Stewart, Charlton Heston, Buster Keaton, and Milton Berle.

THE END OF THE WAR:

I clearly remember the end of the war : It was May 8, 1945, when the war in Europe ended, V-E Day, and a few months later in September of 1945, it was V-J Day. I remember when the news reached our street things went crazy. People cried, shouted, and actually danced in the streets. Soldiers that were in the center of Trenton at the time of the announcement were brought onto our streets to celebrate with all of us. Hastily made dummies of Hitler, Mussolini, and Tajo were quickly made from old clothes and were hung up on the streetlights and burned.

The Gin Mills (neighborhood taverns) were so busy, with large, full containers of beer flowing constantly out the door to folks sitting in front of their homes just celebrating. The years of worry and fear was almost over, we were waiting for the hopeful victory in Japan, which happened in days after the dropping of the atomic bomb. Then the same celebration continued all over the county. War-weary folks were now thinking of homecomings and reunions.

 The service men who were visitors on our street, suddenly found many new, thankful friends and the celebration went on for a few nights. The area churches during that time were overflowing with folks. This also lasted for days.

The days after Japan surrendered were terribly busy. Factories that had geared up to manufacture things for the war effort were starting to reinvent themselves. Products that were forbidden became available to the general public. Foods began to be plentiful. Broadway theaters began gearing up as well, offering all types of entertainment .

 THE FAMILY RELOCATES:

Servicemen and women were returning home, many with "War Brides." Housing was a large problem. New homes were not built anytime during the war and the demand for housing peaked. The Congress of the United States passed a law giving the GI's a guaranteed loan with no money down. Developments started to spring up all over.

Because the country was not use to this new law, Realtors were frightening and timid . So, developers started to build housing in subsidized homes. These were going up and filling amazingly fast.

It was about 1947-1948 when my dad got a great job as supernatant at Leo Roger's homes on Oakland Street. 360 apartments were just being built. Three-story apartments that was going to house many GIs, their war brides, and their kids. There were homes already there, known at the time as the barracks. This is where we lived for the next six years.

They were also going to build two other projects next to these developments, the Willow Homes, and the Haverstock Homes.

It was great. New kids were moving in every day, and we were making new friends. These kids came from all over and were all nationalities.

Many life-long friendships started then, and I still have many great friends I grew up with in those homes. Julie, my future wife, lived in the Donnelly homes.

 For the first time my brothers and sister and I, and all the new kids moving in, really found out that we were poor. We never knew that until we faced our pristine environment among rich and professional folk's children. Now as these new kids were moving in every day, I learned a lesson .

before we moved here, none of us kids ever had a new baseball or baseball bat. We never had a real, official baseball shirt; a real, new football jersey; or ever owned a new baseball glove. We were never the least into these sports, I mean every single day. My sister did with the girls, but never with me .

I remember at that time we would find old, broken, slightly cracked bats and we wrapped black tape around them to straighten them. We used them until they fell apart. We would be taken by the Trenton PAL to Dunn Field to see the Trenton Giants play and sometimes got foul balls or autographed balls. I personally had at least six or seven balls signed by Willie Mays. We never knew he would become famous, so when we needed a ball, we used them. Oh well!

On the streets, we all played a game that sadly is not played today. This game was played by kids like us all over the United States of America. In the fields of Ohio, the coal towns of Pennsylvania, West Virginia, and in the streets of New York. It was called stick ball

Yes, we played baseball or stick ball from the time we got up in the morning until the streetlights went on and it was time to go home .

Each one of us dreamed of becoming a big-league baseball player when we grew up.

Now I for one thought I was great. Yes indeed—old Ed,—me—I was big league stuff. I was sure of that. In the area I lived in at the time, I was considered a skillful player. I honestly believed that too.

So, there are two things you need to know at this point.

1. We kids were meeting new kids every day, because new kids were moving into new homes and apartments nearby.

2. There were many, many new fields for us to play baseball.

So here is when old Ed learned his lesson . You see, it just never entered my mind that these kids moving in also played baseball, and most importantly, I did not realize they also thought they were the best too.

 There was a field right across from where I lived at that time that a few of us started a game on. A few days went by, and as you would imagine, we drew increased kids who wanted to play. Two kids were chosen as captains, and they would pick the team.

Now here comes the crusher: This new gang decided to pick my sister as captain—What???

(I am sure that my sister will not even remember this, but old Ed does—sob, sob, sob.)

Then, my sister, my own sister, who I grew up with, my God she had to know that I was a king—SHE DID NOT CHOOSE HER BROTHER ED—THE BEST BASEBALL PLAYER IN THE ENTIRE WORLD. NO, NO. I was on the other team. The last one picked, mind you! That day I learned that not only was I not as good as I thought, but these new kids were also good, really good. I also found out that my sister—A GIRL—could hit the ball farther than me. No need to tell you, we were beaten badly.

After that, my sister was always picked before me.

I love my sister and always will. But I was humiliated that day. But I did learn a valuable lesson.

After, I would sit on our porch, across from the field, and watch her hit that ball and hear the kids scream. She was a hero.

Yes, my sister was indeed particularly good.

I learned no matter how good and confident you feel in yourself, that there are folks that might have the same goals or dreams as you do in this life. And as good as you feel, no matter what you do, that are there are others just as good as you. The competition is good. That it takes challenging work every single day to accomplish anything worth doing. Nothing, absolutely nothing, is given to you . My dad said it best, he once said, "The best way to get on your feet--is to get off your ass ."

We all soon adjusted to our new surroundings and started school . My siblings and I walked every day first to Gregory School and then later to Jr #3. All the other kids that lived in the surrounding homes all the way up to the Trenton Reservoir walked, and in all kinds of weather. This is where we all discovered Cadwallader Park.

The park offered us children so much all year round. Besides the trees and those great lawns, there was the good old gully on the Stuyvesant Avenue side. We played baseball, football, soccer, and other games there and we would challenge the Donnelly Homes kids, the Chambersburg kids , and other kids to play with us. I tell you; we lost a lot of games there. It was funny because before each game, we would wait for the other teams to arrive to see who we were going to play that day. They came in all sizes: there were big kids, small kids, short kids, and tall kids. We were never sure who we were going to play until after they came. It was what it was, and we tried our best. There were never any fights that I can remember. I became good friends with many guys from the Donnelly homes. In fact, I joined the marines with four of them.

There was a great baseball field across from Jr #3, but the great champions, the American Legion Post #93 Trenton Schroths, played there. We watched them play. The names I remember were Marty Devlin, (he had a brother too), Al Downing (famous New York Yankee pitcher), Chuck Lucarella, Don Pugliese, and Don Palumbo, (all from Chambersburg) and many others.

At Cadwallader, there was the Log Basin, where the folks would all come in the winter for ice skating. There was music and lights and great fun. There were also tennis courts. In the center of the park there were kiddy rides and food concessions owned and operated by the Harrigan Family. They were great folks, and everyone loved them. Great hot days spent there enjoying hamburgers and my favorite RC Cola.

Oh, one other thing you might not know. Behind Jr #3 there was a stream we called "Waterpower." The water flowed down to Stacy Park where the shaky bridge was and emptied into the Delaware River. It was directly across from Jr #threes play yard. There was a big rope on a tree branch that we swung out on and dropped in the water. Today it is known as Route #29. The stream is gone.

There was a teacher from Jr #3 that was always around us, and I remember him as a friend. Pete DeLeon, great man. He loved sports, especially baseball.

Yes, Cadwallader Park became our place to go, to play sports, to hang out.

As we got older, we somehow saved enough money to buy old junk cars and used clunkers. On nice days we religiously ended up in the park, spent hours shining our cars and talking to the other guys. My first car was a green 1939 Plymouth with a rumble seat. Didn't run too well but looked like a new car. It had the white wall "retreads" or "vulcanized tires," as they were known then. We were young but we learned about fixing cars fast and were more than happy to help each other. Gas was about twelve cents a gallon then and the only oil we could get was fifteen cents "Drain Oil."

The daily wardrobe on the summer month's day for guys at that time was jeans, white T-shirts with the cigarettes rolled up and wrapped in the shoulder of one sleeve, and sneakers of some kind.

There was a motorcycle policeman that lived on Woodland Street, which roamed the park and watched us, made sure we cleaned up and acted right. Then there was the famous balloon man at the entrance of the park very Sunday and holidays. It was common for many schools at the end of the year to bring kids in buses to enjoy the park. To see the bears and the monkey . Pew, the smell at times.

Cadwallader Park, at this time in our lives, was a real-to-god wonderful place and a living thing. It was a went on Sundays and holidays. To walk in the park, see the bears, go on the rides, or have a picnic

You could get to the park by bus. Folks came very Sunday from all over Mercer County. The buses ran every fifteen or twenty minutes from Trenton and the surrounding townships.

We all would go to the "Barn," which was the Strand Theater on North Heritage Avenue on Friday nights and then go to the ice cream store across the street.

It was a wonderful time to be young. Our parents and our neighbors made it just that way for us. I know that you might get so tired of hearing about how things were then. But in those long, sizzling summer months, it was wonderful for a teenager with wheels or without wheels. Buses ran from every place in Mercer County and ended up in town. So even without wheels it was easy to get around town.

In the summer months, you wake up and put on your jeans and T-shirt with the cigarettes rolled up in your sleeves. Then you'd jump on a bus and head into town: for a new adventure, to hang out, to buy some new forty-fives, walk around, meet the gang or new kids, stop at Kresge's, Murphy's, or Sears for a soda. Then maybe I would meet the gang somewhere and have lunch, then sometimes we would go the movies at the State Theater, the Stacy, the Capital, the Trent, or the Lincoln. All of them advertised chilly air conditioning.

The times when we were broke, but didn't want to head home, we could just stand around on State and Broad Street at noon and see the buses coming and going. Smell the aroma of those wonderful and fanatic scents of Planter Peanuts roasting. There were always kids we knew downtown for some reason.

In those days there were no shopping centers; Downtown was where it was. On Thursday nights, the town was open until nine and we kids drove the Trenton Police nuts, just driving around and around shouting at the girls. You might read this and think it was crazy , but all those crazy things we did are such wonderful memories to a lot of us. Going into town is why I had a paper route, why I cut grass, why I washed cars, or shined shoes.

I would like to say that in those days, we kids didn't need dope. We all got high on new days, music, dancing, going downtown, cars, and of course those wonderful girls. One blanket could be a lot of fun. Picnics in the park or lying on the beach. Or laying on the lawn at night when it was quiet, just holding hands looking at the stars.

After one of us got wheels, we reached out. We went to drive-in restaurants and drive-in movies. Wow, a dollar a carload. I remember late at night driving to Philadelphia to go to the Horn and Haricot restaurant. Some nights we would all hang out in the parks around Trenton.

The big treat and the big events were saved for the weekends. The dances. Those wonderful, unforgettable dances. We all had favorite places to go.

It was great. We all went on to other things, but we had a ball in those years. With little money, no wheels , and with the permission and their blessing of our parents.

Here is a day in my life I wish so share. It's June, I am seventeen years old. Like a lot of kids in those days, I quit school in the seventh grade and lied about my age and got a job in the service department of CV Refrigeration Company. I was making $1.10 an hour, which was good money in those days. At this time, I bought a lot of clothes.

Now I need to tell you that at this time I was not into learning. I was a bad student. I have always been an observer and listener. It seems that somehow, I could comprehend and understand things, even though it was the truth that I could not read or spell too well. It would be like this the rest of my life.

At this time, I would like to express something that is especially important to understand and is part of my main reason for this story and shall become a principal factor in my life in the coming future.

Also, I would like to point out that it has always been my belief that the children that were born and lived through the depression and the war years, without realizing it, matured faster than the children after us. We had to.

I honestly believe that even though I had little education, I would, in my life, have the strange ability to clearly understand the meaning of words, large words. Despite that fact that I would not be able to spell or maybe recognize the word. All my life I have loved words and their meaning.

A DAY IN MY LIFE:

It was hot so I spent the afternoon at Cadwallader Park with the guys laying on the grass and giving cars another wax job with turtle wax. My car is cleaned, and I am happy with the new checker-box seat covers that I bought for $19.95 from Sears Auto Seat Covers Shop. My car now looks sharp.

We're going tonight to the dance at Prospect Street Presbyterian Church. This is only one of the many places we could go, but we like it here. I hurried home because I had some things to do. First, I checked my dark-blue pegged pants. Shine my black penny loafers. I picked out of the wash one of my sharpest, blue, short-sleeved shirts and got out the iron and ironing board. I iron it really good. Hang it on the hanger and go take my shower.

After putting a little wild-root hair cream on my hair, I bush it into a DA (Ducks Ass), I splash on some Blue Velvet, and I am ready.

I pull up and find a place to park in an area where kids are going to see my shining car. The dance hall is in the back section of the church, in the basement area. I see a bunch of kids hanging around the door, say my hello's and walk in. The dance hall is dimly lit. All around the walls are nothing but those church folding chairs.

Once inside I am greeted by one of the adult chaperones.

The dance has started, there is a slow song on, "Sixteen Candles." There are few couples on the floor yet. I look around the room and I see the same arrangements I see at all dances. It seems like we act like fish in a bowl sometimes. All the girls sitting together in one spot, the boys in another, a scatter of couples standing around just holding hands and more kids arriving.

I talked to the guys, looked around to see who I knew, and who I could dance with first. I was a great slow dancer and liked to think I could jitterbug or fast dance fairly good.

I always love to remember just looking at the girls and the smells. Mm. A few things I remember very well. In the winter months—those six-button Benny. Always their hair. Wow, they did things with their hair. I of course adored ponytails. Then there was those jeans and OMG don't ever forget what they wore on their feet—even in the snow—ballerina slippers. They looked so great. And were at every dance.

During these dances, there were a lot of boys and girls that were bashful and very timid, and they sat around a lot, with their friends trying to encourage them. I can tell you that these dances were a wonderful place for these kids to blossom and many did just that. You could see one of them one week sitting all alone, two weeks later out there on the floor having a ball.

Whoever they picked to play the records was great. They always played the newest and most popular and mixed the slow dances with fast dances. I always remembered that after the dances we would all want to go someplace to eat. Many kids would hop in the cars of guys like me and head off into the night for a new adventure.

Many of you Trenton folk will not remember, but there was a Parkway Diner just off of Prospect Street behind CV Hills and Westinghouse. That is where we went at that time. We would follow each other to the diner, go inside, and find a booth next to other booths of the gang. We would have our cokes and hamburgers, and, of course, many French fries.

It seems that the owners and waitresses at that time were so cool. They let us stay, I guess longer, as long as we were not loud and showed respect to the other customers.

After we would break up and go outside. It's in the parking lot, leaning against the cars, we would talk long into the night, until one-by-one, we would leave.

NATIONAL GUARD ADVENTURE:

It must be remembered that there was no fast-food restaurants at this time. There were drug stores, coffee shops, and some diners.

It is a sizzling summer night. My friend Frank and I are standing in front of a jukebox listening to music at the Rendezvous Restaurant on Pennington Avenue. At the time I was about fourteen-and-half years old. Just then a man, who was a neighbor of the restaurant, walked up to us and said, "Why don't you guys join the National Guard?"

Frank and I looked at each other. This guy thinks we are seventeen, we both thought at the time. Before we could answer, he said, "Come with me." He took us outside and sat us in a yellow Plymouth convertible with the top down and started to drive us to the 50th Armored Division's building on Eggert's Crossing Road.

It was a beautiful night, and I enjoyed the ride. He took us in, showed us rifles, pistols, tanks, trucks, uniforms, and gave us both an application to join. Then took us back.

Frank and I were mystified and impressed. We had never ever seen any of that before and to think he took us for seventeen, which was the age you needed to be, only also with your parent's signed permission.

It was then we both did a crazy thing: We signed our mother's name.

We got a friend to drive us up on the day they wanted us. He waited outside. They swore us in, then issued us a complete uniform, with shoes, boots, and a helmet liner with the 50th Armored insignia on it.

We then were assigned to the same company, and we went to monthly meetings there. At the first meeting we met Johnny. who, as it happens, lived not far from us, and offered us a ride home? After which, he would take us back and forth from our meetings. We, unbelievably, were accepted by the guys and made new friends with all the older men. If anyone ever suspected that we were underage, they never said anything about it.

It was not long before my parents discovered what I had done. They both wanted to kill me. They didn't know what to do. They feared that I could be in store for a bout of trouble. But they were afraid to do anything, and I convinced them to just let it be. That no one might ever discover it. So very reluctantly, they remained silent.

Frank and I went in a caravan of trucks to Pine Camp or Lake Drum, NY, twice. We went on maneuvers with the guys, rode in tanks, trucks, and did KP duty.

At sixteen, we now joined the troops to drink beers and visited the Black River Café many times.

All this time we were still going to school. I was not a good student. For the Guard, we were required at times to march or be in the different parades that Trenton offered then. In uniform.

The day finally came. Frank and I were sitting in the back of an army five-ton truck passing the Hotel Stacy Trent when we were spotted by our gym teacher.

He reported us and we were court martialed and both were given a General Discharge Under Honorable Conditions, by which my mother and I were surprised. This is a good honorable discharge.

MEETING JULIE AND JOINING THE MARINES:

After that I joined the Marine Corps and was sent to Parris Island, South Carolina. We arrived early in the morning. There were 188 men in the original platoons, but only eighty-three of us made it through and graduated. I graduated with Private First-Class Strips, only ten in the platoon received them.

Those thirteen weeks I survived there was the greatest test as a man that I ever had. It is said, and I swear by it, that if you can make it through the

Marine Boot Camp, then you can make it through anything.

The Korean War was on when I enlisted but was over when I graduated. So, I was stationed in Camp Lejeune, North Carolina, and in Philadelphia, Boston, Portsmouth, and New Hampshire.

I was home on leave and about to return when I met Julie who was 13 years of age and as pretty as could be, at that time, I was seventeen, She loved my Marine dress uniform, I left knowing that I would never see this young girl again, but for some reason she stay with me, and she had a large effect on the poems. I thought about her a lot "Puppy Love?" I never knew,. But there was an effect on me, It was here that my love for words blossomed. As a kid during the war about six years old, whenever I heard an adult say a word, I would ask what that word meant and they would tell me, now at 6 years old I could pronounce the word and knew it's meaning, but I could not read or write. Then an age 9 I found that I could rhyme words, I then loved music and hoped to be a song writer someday. I honestly believe that for some reason, even though I had little education, I would, in my life, have the strange ability to clearly understand the meaning of words, large words, despite that fact that I would not be able to spell or maybe recognize the word. All my life, I have loved words and their meaning. I heard the words in all those love songs that blared out of the jukeboxes and radios.

In the 1950s one of my favorite groups was Al Alberts and the Four Aces (Al later would became friends) . As a teen, we would stand on the corner or get in a stairwell of a building to sing and harmonize their songs. In later years, Al and his wife Stella would become friends with Julie and me.

I started to write poetry. I thought that I could write, and I dreamed about being a songwriter. I could sing well too. But even though I could not spell or read too well, I could write, and I was good at making words rhyme.

In the Marines, while far away from home and mostly around Christmas holidays, I became known around the barracks and to many of my fellow marines as the guy that could write romantic stuff.

Soon I was writing for them, and they would take my romantic poems and send them or give them to their loved ones. They were saying that they wrote them themselves. I had no problem with that. If fact, it made me happy to write for them. I have no idea how many I wrote and gave them to each person Free

I was away from home, homesick, and just a crazy, young, mixed-up, romantic guy. Like all guys, I hoped that I would someday find the girl of my dreams. For me, all the poems for others was as if I was writing just to that one-in-a-million girl.

Still in the Marines, on Christmas Eve 1953 I went to midnight mass, I returned to the gent, it was bitter cold, I was so down I felt so low, was I homesick?, scared? Or what. I had been thinking of this young exceptionally pretty girl and I wrote these two poems, knowing all the time that I would never see her again/

unknown reason, every By this time, I knew a lot of girls , but for some time I wrote something after that, when I would reread it to myself, I saw her in my mind. Now, I must confess that I was not smart enough to know the workings of God, but this was part of his plan. There was just something about her that from time-to-time while writing and drinking, even though I never thought that I would see her again and did not see her again for years, her face was with me as I wrote. Silly I know , but it is true.

That Christmas, she became the inspiration and stimulation for two poems I wrote. Once again it was her face that caused this. I would keep these and many years later, I would give them to her and tell her that these were written and meant for my Julianne, the girl of my dreams. Julie loved them both.

The first was:

I closed my eyes and there you are

You're always on my mind

I think about you through the day

And through the night I find

You're always with me darling

I see you standing there

With the sunlight dancing

Though your lovely auburn hair

I see your eyes sparkle

They sometimes seem to dance

And when I look into them

They put me in a trance

I'd rather have you here with me

Then have you on my mind

Cause you'll never really know my dear

The happiness I find.

The second one was:

Because some day, I hope and pray

To take you for my wife

And if someday, God finds a way

To make my dreams come true

To give me my biggest prize in life

My darling which is you

Boy, was I crazy for her,

All my friends love them both, . So, I had a friend, Larry, help me. I was really looked-up to and because of my ability. I was by him, and many others encouraged me to become a songwriter, which was something I always wanted to do. But I was frustrated to the point that I drank a lot—really a lot— and got into trouble.

An example (12/24/1953

I remember riding in a jeep going to a motor compound with a friend of mine from Jessup, Georgia. He asked me to write a love poem for his girl Sandy. I had never seen her or a picture, but this is what I wrote on an old box top in about fifteen minutes:

S- Is for the sweetest girl I know.

A- Is for the answer to my dreams.

N- Is for the neatness of her figure.

D- Is for the dear she is to me.

Y- Is for the yearning I have for her.

Each and every day that we're apart-

Put them all together, they spell SANDY:

a name tattooed in my heart.

I drafted many poems for many marines.

While drinking and being so young and always writing about love and marriage, I too wondered what kind of girl might be interested in me. I was homesick and lonely without telling anyone.

Since I was stationed down south or often stationed with southern boys, my love for country music was on fire.

Back when I was fourteen, I discovered what was known then as "hillbilly music," which is known today as country music. Now, growing up at that time, if you liked that type of music you were considered kind of strange. So, it followed that there were few radio stations that played country music.

The two most popular where WCKY in Cincinnati, Ohio, and the other one was dubbed the WWVA in Wheeling, West Virginia. So, at fourteen years old, that's when I fell in love with Hank Williams forever.

BAD YEARS:

Anyway, I was discharged from the marines, and I didn't want to work right away. I roamed all over, drinking and hanging out down by the shore .I still wrote and wanted to pursue writing songs. I adore music and words; I am sure more that anyone knows. But I didn't know what to do. I could not play an instrument, but hung around, drinking with many, and could be found all over the place.

After I returned home, I was a bum. I really was. I was living anyplace I could and just going from job-to-job, drinking a lot of scotch and water, and throwing back beers. Depressed at times, I was just a mess in those years. Doing things, I shouldn't. (Don't ask.)

I battled with the problem of not being able to read or write. Because of this, I had a feeling inside that my poems were not good. To a point where I would write, with all the misspelled words , then get drunk and rip them up.

Then I got a job, but I was still partying and coming in drunk at all hours of the morning. Now, my mom had a rule that you had to be in before midnight, which I broke all the time. She soon gave me a choice to stay and obey the rules or leave. By not coming home before midnight, she said I was setting a bad example for my brothers.

So, things got crazy for the next few years. I had many jobs, many cars, and many drinks. I slept in many places, at many friend's houses. I was well on my way to being a good bum.

During this time, I wrote hundreds of poems for songs and got offers to write for many publishers: Tin Pan Alley Publishers, Music Master Publishing Company, Jewel Music Masters, and others. I never thought I was good at this, which apparently, I was.

The 1950s music seemed to be never-ending and was romantic and new songs were being written every week. There was a show outside of New York on WOR called the Make-Believe Ballroom. I listened to it all the time. It was a wonderful show and played all the newest and best songs. The music was fantastic. I can tell you that I grew up in a world much different than yours. It really was.

The 1940s and 1950s were the most romantic times ever. All the music and movies will show you that, all the love songs and the words to the music at that time. Most of it was for and about young lovers. Teenagers and folks in their twenties. The greatest singers, both male and female, were recording love songs each week. Each song was filled with all the world's best-known love words. Love, feelings, and words. Words, words.

And of course, there was also Rock and Roll. But we all, and I mean all, loved to slow dance and hold our partners.

I was now twenty years old and had been living a crazy life. But now I had to come to my senses. I loved writing, but it seemed to me that it was never meant to be. Writing made me drink, it made me a bum, and my education problems both depressed me and convinced me that I was just not good enough. So slowly I stopped and moved back home with mom.

 I was living at home, and I got a steady job .

MEETING JULIE FOR THE FIRST TIME— MY LIFE BEGINS:

I traveled around after I was discharged for a years or two, then I came home and safter a few days I went for lunch at a favorite restaurant and as I was eating the door opened and there was Julie, Wow, It had been three years. Was that really her? I could not believe it. I had never dreamed that I would ever see her again, even though her face was always in my mind. But there she was. I saw just how beautiful had become since I had last seen her.

It seems that she was now seventeen and had a summer job working for New Jersey Tobacco on Prospect Street, four blocks away. She started to come to Susan's for lunch every day, with an older Italian lady named Rose that she worked with. Of course, I noticed her, she was a beautiful teenage girl, and I would sit with them, and a few times paid for their lunches.

I was devastated and did not know just what to do, for sure by now I knew that I cared a lot for her.

So rollickingly I went to her table, I was more nervous than I could remember, and she said, "Eddie when did you come home?"

This is what came out of me, I was so freckling nervous, I stood there and said.

"Angels never leave haven

At least that's what I been told

So how did you get here on earth for some to have and hold

I know I can find the answer to that Julie+

Because I was sit there with you

I'd put my arms around you

And I would be in heaven too."

The customers all overheard me and applause

That was just how it happened.

I asked her for a date:

Soon I asked her to go to the Steele Pier in Atlantic City, it was a great warm sunny July day that I will always remember.

We double dated her friend, and I found out that once dated her older sister Millie. She had a sister four years younger than her named Ada. That was where I first met my future bride.

Ada and Julianne had grown up together, and they all went to school together. Now at the time of this visit, I was about seventeen and she was thirteen. I was told that she had a crush on me, but to me at that time, she was just a kid. Of course, over a period of time, going over there I saw her many times.

Later during the next few days, for some reason, I thought of her. She had a special glow about her, a youthful freshness and innocence that for some reason intrigued me. To this day I have no idea why, but it just did. This had never happened to me before and would never happen again in my life. The words of a poem formed in my head as I saw her young face. It went like this:

It was funny, because as I was writing these eight simple lines, all the while I was picturing the face of this young girl that had a crush on me, Julianne.

One night pulled out the two poems that I wrote for her, telling me that when I wrote them for her when I had no thoughts of seeing her again, she cried when she read them. I said, when I gave them to her, I told Julie that I had been dreaming of her for a long time and wrote these for her. But I know that the words used in both poems were about her even before we married. Julianne was, and will always be, the girl of my dreams.

I used to hang out, mostly at lunchtime, at a restaurant on Prospect Street called Susan's. There were no McDonald's or any fast-food places then, just sweet shops and restaurants. Susan's was a few blocks from my home on Exton Avenue and all my friends went there for lunch or to hang out.

At that time, before we met again, I was a great dresser, or a "Dapper," and worked at a million different jobs for clothes. But wherever I lived, no matter where, I washed and ironed my pants and shirts. I loved clothes at this time. All the girls and women at the Restaurant loved to read my poems and would make copies to take to work and show other folks. I wrote a lot, and after I wrote them, I would get stone drunk and tear them up . I was a mess.

I was a total romantic at this time. As I look back now, I can see that I was just a young, mixed-up guy and the poems I wrote were for and about the girl that I dreamed someday of finding, marrying, and settling down with a girl like Julie. Just like all guys and girls. I was no different, I only had the talent to write and compose.

Now up to this time, just before I met Julie again and she came back into my world, I was working, off and on, I still was a total mess, I drank, and I didn't care about anything .

My family or anyone that knew me and might have read this could never understand how bad I felt at this time. Nor would they understand that it was Julie that really saved me and turned both my thinking and my world around.

After all these years and life, I had found Julie , she was my angel: This was so unreal the way it really happened.

Who would ever think that one day at Susan's that we would be reacquainted. I knew Julie did not drive. She was seventeen and still in school and was to graduate in June.

She had to take wo buses to come to work, and to go home, or she got a ride from someone. It was summer and this was a summer job that became full-time later on.

I started to be there when she finished work and took her home. ,Suddenly I found myself at her house at eight in the morning to take her to work.

Our first real date was to Atlantic City's Steel Pier. The second was a movie, then to the Friday night dances in Trenton at Donnelly Homes. There were dances all over Trenton in those days. Ada had a boyfriend Louie, We doubled-dated with Louie and Ada a lot. Ada was liked a sister to Julie. Julie and Louie could really dance together .

It was not long before deep inside me, I realized that the words I had written so many years ago were about her. After all these years, she was the girl of my dreams that I longed for so much. It was absolutely true that I did write them especially for her. I realized, again deep inside, God—she was the one I was thinking of. That I would ever meet her again and these words would ever mean anything to her. Julie was the girl of my dreams that I always wanted and the exact girl I was thinking about when I wrote these. All our lives .

Soon, we were going steady, and she got me to keep one job and I worked every day. I moved back home with Mom, and I followed her rules. I stopped drinking my scotch and water. Julie had changed me. I felt so much better about myself. I was on longer a bum. I started to work for Remmert-Werner at Mercer Airport. I needed the money to take her out. She became my life. Time went by so fast. I knew she was getting serious—too serious. She would sit close to me and hold my hand wherever we went. Julie was, at all times, a hand holder. Even just sitting in the car driving or on the couch.

God knows the truth; she was just so damn gorgeous. The other guys would look and stare at her all the time. That made me mad and very jealous. She looked good, smelled wonderful, but was very shy with other people.

I remember the first time I took her home to meet my family. I can tell you my mother and dad loved her instantly.

She would graduate from Saint Mary's and was now working full-time. Slowly she started to drop little hints. Ada and Louie were getting married.

"Hum. "she said. I knew what she meant. But I didn't want to be rushed or to get married.

I knew that she was serious and at that time, I was definitely not ready. To tell the truth, I did not think I was good enough for her. I had no education, I still could not read or spell too well, and had no money. I thought she could do better than me. But I couldn't tell her that.

So, one day I wrote her a long letter. I guess I didn't have the guts to tell her in person. I sent it to her house in the mail. In it I told her, in at least seven or ten diverse ways, that it was over, I was

done, I didn't want to see her again—
Just leave me alone. But as you will see,
she would not let me be.

Julie returns:

Sure, as hell, a few days later I was at
Susan's at noon and she came in, said
hello to everyone, and sat close to me.
As she always did, she took my hand. I
just looked at her. I knew she had
received the letter, but it blew my mind
that she was here.

So, surprised I said, "Did you get my
letter?"

"Yep," she said, looking at me.

Well, didn't you understand it?" I
asked.

"Yep," she said again.

Then she took both of my hands ,
looked me in the eyes, and said, "I read
what you said, Eddie—But I know you
didn't mean a word you wrote. Because

no one can say I love you better than you."

Julie saw something in me. After that, I knew she loved me. My world had changed for the better. After that, we saw each other every single day. We were inseparable. However, Julie was still not really sure I would not write another letter or change my mind about her. We then both fell deeply in love with Joni James, her songs, but mostly the words. We wore that record out.

 She loved the song "Little Things Mean A Lot" and would sing it to me as we danced. She wanted to send me a message I suppose. (Listen to the song please, you will hear the words.) The key words were *"You don't have buy me diamonds or pearls...I never cared much for diamonds and pearls, cause honestly, honey, they just cost money."*

We had just started talking about marriage and the wedding at this time. She was telling me to forget about having a big wedding, which I was thinking hard about at the time.

To convince her I loved her, when we danced, I sang to her the other great Joni James song, "Why Don't You Believe Me." The key words were *"Here is a heart that is lonely. Here is a heart you can take. Here is a heart for you only, that you can keep or break. How else can I tell you? What more can I do? Why don't you believe me, I love only you?"* This was my message back to her and I couldn't have written better words to tell her. It was meant for her. (If you ever get the opportunity, listen to the songs and the words please.)

 We both enjoyed all romantic songs, loved them. Joni James seemed to be singing our words and how we felt. We both would listen and hear the songs, the words, and the real feelings we felt. We would just sit and listen to music for hours. Drive around at night, park, and just listen.

I remember Julie singing and dancing with our children when they were little. They might not remember her singing, but she did. We started having our children listen to music at an early age. A lot of Hank Williams and Burl Ives's "Little White Duck." As a result, in later years Michael, David, and Eddie would all learn to play guitars and other musical instruments. All of our children would in later years love music as Julie and I did.

Planning:

Then we really fell more deeply in love. We started to plan; we even bought a house full of furniture at the Olden House on Olden Avenue on the layaway program, making payments each month. Our bedroom set was one.

We really wanted to get married, however we had no money. Our parents didn't have any either. We did not want to burden them, so we knew it had to be a small wedding.

Julie just wanted to run away to Elton, Maryland, were for years you could get married at sixteen without your parent's permission . She didn't want to start off in debt, weddings were expensive.

Julie didn't want to spend money. Although I knew she was right, still somehow, I knew this would be very wrong, I knew that she went to Saint Mary's Cathedral and most of her friends had been married there.

I knew that every girl dreamed of having a church wedding and I wanted her to have her "Big Wedding."

But she said no many times. But I felt deep inside that even though she knew we could not afford it; I knew she really wanted it badly.

So, at the time it was a constant obsession with me *not* to marry *my wife without giving her that wedding I knew that she and all young girls dreamed of having.* I had to give it to her. I felt that maybe five, or ten, or thirty years down the road, she would feel sad and regret that we didn't have a big wedding. I knew somehow, I had to find a way.

We were both at our great friends Louie and Ada's wedding. One day I was talking to Ada, who wanted to know when we were going to get married, and I told her what I wanted. Ada volunteered right then that Julie could use her wedding dress. They had the same dress size, with just some small alterations. This was Ada, as unselfish as she had always been. Ada's kind offer set off ideas in my head. It was true that Ada and Julie were almost the same size. God bless Ada. She and Louie were especially important in all this.

I set out with a plan, without Julie knowing, and I set our wedding up.

Pictures—At the time, I had a good friend and neighbor who was a photographer for Howard Studio's, they were the biggest and the best wedding photographers in Trenton. He offered that if I were short money that he could take all the pictures at cost, and I could pay him whenever I could. Wow!

Music—A good friend had a teen band that played for nothing at our wedding.

Hall & Food—I had an idea—

Understand I knew nothing about weddings, I just knew it was free food, free drinks, music , dancing, and girls . So, on a Sunday morning, I went to see a guy I knew, Al.

He owned the Villa Capri Hall on Phillips Avenue. He also owned Al's Tavern in East Trenton. Over the years, I had gotten to know him well.

I remember it was a sizzling summer day. Al was cleaning up after a big wedding from the day before and had the big fans going. All the doors and windows were open.

I walked in and he shouted, "Eddie, what the hell do you want?" Al was a great kidder. Told him I was getting married. He went nuts. "Are you crazy kid? Are you out of your mind?"

I started to help him clear the tables from a wedding the day before and I did that for about an hour, but Al sensed that something was yup, so he stop me, looked in my eyes and said "So, what do you want from me, Ed?"

I choked up and stuttered out for what I came there. I said, "I don't have the money for a wedding right now. I wanted to know if there is a way that you can allow us to use this hall, you cater the wedding, and I can pay you later."

Al then went really crazy. He busted a bottle, threw a few chairs, and went into his office screaming how crazy I was. I sat there alone by myself with the fans blowing.

I sat there for a long while. There was no noise, just the sound of the fan and the sound of cars off in the distance. After about fifteen minutes, I got up to go and shouted, "See you later Al. Sorry I asked you."

Then there was a shout. "Eddie, get our ass in here," he shouted. "Get in here now." I walked into his office, and he had his appointment book open. He looked at me and said, "I got September the 10th open." I was shocked.

Al smiled at me and said, "The cost to you will be a buffet for two dollars a person, which includes food and one-hour open bar." Then he wanted to know how many people would come. I didn't have a clue.

Al laughed and said, "You crazy bastard. You're getting married and don't know how many folks you have. Ed, I have penciled you in, now get out of here." While I was leaving, he said, "And if you don't pay, I'm going to send an ugly, big guy to collect." This kind of guy was known as the local "Enforcer."

Then it hit me. God, now that I have the hall and that was Al's only date open. Oh, what if Saint Mary's Cathedral was booked that day? That was the only reason I did all this. If the church was not available on that date, then I would have to cancel it all.

So, I rushed to Saint Mary's and found the monsignor working in the yard. Told him what I had done and what I needed. He walked us into his office, and Yes, to my joy, September 10th was free. I then asked the monsignor if he would marry us on that day. He had known my mom since she was a child and said he would be more than happy to do it. Wow! Wow! I did it—I think—now I have to convince Julie. I knew that was not going to be an easy thing.

I break the news"

That night I took Julie to a drive-in movie and went I thought it was the right time, I very slowly told her what I had done. She was so mad she started to cry, and she got out of the car. I could not find her. I looked and looked for an hour, I even walked out to the street. Where was she, where did she go? I looked far down both sides of the road. Did she flag a cab? Or a bus? She was nowhere. Not knowing what to do, or where she went, I went back and waited in the car until she returned.

When she returned, Julie was still crying and terribly upset and really mad. She said, "Eddie. We don't have money and you want to start our life off in debt. You have no idea what this will cost."

Still very mad, she told me to take her home, which I did. She just jumped out of the car when we got there. She would not answer the phone or come out to talk to me when I went to her house. She was indeed very mad.

Three days later:

She then called me and asked me to cancel all of it, but I wanted to do it. I convinced her that things would be all right . I promised that I would get a second job and pay it off, but I wanted her to have this wedding. Very, very slowly she agreed. It was set! This really was going to happen. I am going to marry my love. Wow!

Before we married, I had a problem that I really needed and wanted to see if I could solve. It is an incredibly special story for me, one that to this day I am extremely proud of myself and my bride Julie for doing. At the end of this story I will explain why.

I came from a large, loving family. Nine children. My Dad and Mom never drove a car. When we were kids, Mom took us shopping with her and we either carried bags of food or used a big red wagon.

Mom had a bad right wrist; she could not bend it at all. She needed help a lot. As we got older, and had cars, Mom would ask one of us to take her shopping.

But Mom was a person who didn't like to bother anyone. Sometimes, she would not ask someone to drive her, but would take that wagon and go by herself. Even if we told her it was OK, she was stubborn in many ways. She didn't want to bother us.

Julie and I took her shopping and to the doctor a lot. But we knew that when we married, we would be living in Pennsylvania for a while. It bothered me that Mom would not ask people for help.

At the time I was working up at Mercer Airport and I had a big Old's '98. So, one night Julie and I took Mom to dinner, and we ended up on the tarmac of the airport. As you can imagine, it was very dark there. I got out of the car and somehow, I still don't know how, I got Mom to sit in the driver's seat.

 After a series of "No, Ed, No, Ed, No Ed," I got into the passenger side and showed Mom that I could control the steering and brakes from where I was. I then told her to drive a little, that there was no one here, and there was nothing to hit. She hollered and hollered, but I kept on coaching her to just go a little bit, please Mom, step on the gas, and just drive a little bit.

 "No, No, Eddie, stop it" she said over and over again. But I didn't until she drove about two thousand feet. I stopped the car.

Mom got in the back seat; she was mad—burning mad.

I started home. Julie said nothing, nor did I. Nothing but silence filled the car.

 Then. Mom said, "I didn't do bad, did I? That was fun. "WOW! Mom wanted to learn. WOW! After that, Julie and I took Mom out every day and taught her how to drive. Now it is important to tell you my mom was fifty-three years old at that time. All her life she had to depend on others to take her place. Because she was so stubborn, most of her life was spent within the four walls of our home. My mom loved Julie and felt close to her so Julie took her to take her driver's test. She passed.

Now it seems that no one, not even Mom, told my Dad or the family what she was doing, and it came as a total shock to them all. My dad said, "Eddie, you are going to get your mother killed." But the deed was done. Mom bought a car and then started to drive herself to work and to go shopping.

My family was not incredibly happy with Julie or me and told us so:... "Mom is going to get hurt;" "You don't know what you have done;" "You put our mother in harm's way."

Then one day Mom called and said, "Eddie, guess where I drove to today." She said that she took my younger brother and sister with her.

I said, "Where Mom?"

She answered. "Seaside Heights, and yesterday I drove to Norristown, PA." She went on the busy Pennsylvania turnpike by herself.

I could not believe it, but Mom loved to drive and was particularly good at it.

Now to tell you all why I love this so much. Mom was a lady that never went anywhere, and I mean she went nowhere, unless someone offered and drove her. Mom yearned to go difference places, see different things, and not depend on anyone, or to be forced to wait until someone was ready to take her. Mom wanted to enjoy the rest of her life.

Mom and Julie are with God now. It might not be an important thing to many, but I say once again, I am proud of what my bride and I did. Without realizing it at the time, Julie and I really helped Mom become free.

Free for the first time in her life. You could tell just by talking to her, she loved this new freedom. Don't get me wrong, Mom loved her life and all her children and grandchildren, but she needed something else, to be independent.

God, she did not have to wait, put off, or ask anyone to take her. She just drove herself. Because of this newfound freedom, my Mom took art classes, and became a particularly good artist. She visited her friends at their homes and in the hospital, could visit her children, and shopped whenever she wanted to.

You know, we forget sometimes that we are incredibly lucky, and we all just take driving, and coming and going as we please, as if it's nothing big or exciting. But to someone like my mom, it was a release she needed. I had taken care of Mom and was now getting ready for Julie and my big day. Our wedding.

THE BIG DAY ARRIVES:

The day finally came, September 10, 1960,Saint Mary's Cathedral.

I remember on our wedding day; I was getting dressed in my tuxedo when all of a sudden, I got a chill. Things were going through my head: Did I really want to get married? That lousy feeling that she was too good for me, crept back into my mind once more. This is an excessively big responsibility! Was I ready for this? Did I really love Julie? Love her enough to live with her all my life? Am I good enough for her?

Then my mind switched to the wedding reception and the cost: Was Julie, right? Did I take on more than I might be able to manage? Am I making a big mistake starting our life off in debt? We really did not have the money to do this. We were starting our lives off with some tension. What if I can't pay for the reception? This was really a large gamble. I felt sick and my nerves were bad. I knew that Julie was unhappy and scared because I forced her to go along with me.

I can tell you; I was more than nervous as I was standing at the altar. Then the organ started playing "Here Comes the Bride." The church was full. I stood there, looked up at the ceiling of that magnificent church, and then my eyes slowly, very slowly, dropped down to her as I watched the bridesmaids and her father walk her up to the altar.

As she reached me, and her father handed her over, the light and the soft rays of sun shone down from the windows on her and that beautiful white gown. She looked so radiant, so damn beautiful, and she glowed for a slight moment. I was breathless for a second; she looked like an angel. To me, at that second, there never was in history a more beautiful bride than mine.

Right after her father lifted her veil and kissed her, I took her hand, and I made her look at me and I whispered to her, not really caring that folks might be looking or listening. I looked deep in her eyes while I held her hand and said, "Julie, are you sure you want this-are you sure?"

I remember the look she gave me, and she said, "Yes, yes, yes. Eddie, I love you."

 Then, out of nowhere, I seemed to realize at once that I adored her more than anything in life. I felt that I would do anything for her. I knew that we might never be rich, but we would have a wonderful life. I felt an overwhelming feeling that we would be OK That no matter what this woman loved me. This all happened in church on our wedding day, so it had to be right, I thought. I would try to be a great husband.

For that split second in that church, I need you to know that I felt so exceptionally lucky to be marrying this angel. She was my bride. I thought really, she was too good for me. God!

It was faith that somehow, long before I met her, she was indeed that girl I had been writing and dreaming about for so long. The same girl I did not think I was worthy of, and on this day, I was marrying her.

Our wedding day was great. Great weather and we were so much in love.

We rode in the cars to the park, took all the typical pictures, and then went to the hall. It was a warm, sunny day and we were both surprised at all the people that attended. We had no idea how many folks would come. Frankie and his band were particularly good. As always, the young kids loved the music and the older folks said it was too loud.

Julie was so happy so many of her friends had come. The girls she went to school with were there. We danced and welcomed all our guests. All our family and friends were there. Seeing the look on Julie's face, I felt a sense of happiness and was immensely proud that I gave Julie this wonderful wedding. We danced and talked all day. There were large circular fans in the hall, and one had sucked Julie's long veil into it. I grabbed her and the veil went into the blades.

 BACK AT THE HALL.

At this point, I want to remind you once again that from the start I really didn't know much about weddings. I knew nothing about them when I first talked to Al. I knew nothing about the protocol and what happens at them. I had been to only a few weddings, and as a wild kid, all I ever knew was that there was free drinks, food, girls, and dancing.

It was then that I noticed something that I totally knew nothing about and never expected. Julie had this white bag and all during the reception folks were giving us envelopes. It was not that I had forgotten, I simply did not know that folks give money as wedding presents. We were getting money. Our wonderful friends, parents, and relatives gave us cards and funds for our future.

It was getting late, and we were supposed to leave on our honeymoon. But since we had the envelopes and Julie was so nervous about making sure we paid Al before we left the hall. I said, "Let's wait; we'll pay him tomorrow." But she had that bag full of wedding envelopes and she felt it might contain enough to pay him before we left.

I never dreamed we would be able to pay Al, but we did. So, Julie in her gown and me in my tuxedo went into Al's office and opened the envelopes one-by–one. I recorded the amount given on each envelope. Sure enough, after counting the money, not only did we have enough, but there was some left over.

My dad, at this time, was a drinking friend with many politicians. One was Trenton Mayor Donald J. Connolly. They had their own drinking party in the back of the hall near the bar. He gave us a gift, which was a fortune at that time. I remember the total bill we paid was even more that I had originally figured. Wow, we had a lot of folks there.

Now, you need to know we both didn't think we would have enough money for everything, but we were a bit ashamed and didn't want folks to know that we had no money.

We lied and told everyone that we were going to the Mountains on our honeymoon, it was even published in both Trenton newspapers, when in fact after the reception, we went to the house we rented and furnished In Levittown, PA. We didn't leave the house for three days. This story of how we got married, I far as I know in our fifty-three years of marriage, I don't think we ever once told anyone about it. This was one most important day in my life, including the day I met Julie again at Susan's. I think now it's that one day in a lifetime, that I discovered true love.

THE FAMILY BEGINS:

Our life was wonderful. We were so much in love. it was September 25, 1961, that our first daughter Shari was born. We were so happy. But then as we had known and accepted there was a work labor problem and my company closed and moved to Ohio. I was out of work. Julie had just given birth, I wanted her to stay at home. Our lease was up so we moved back to Trenton in a second-floor apartment across from her parents for a short while. Then we got a rental, a two-bedroom house in the Donnelly homes, where our son Michael was born.

 I went back to driving a cab , which was something Julie didn't want because I worked at night. The truth is I made much more money daily than I would have working in a factory at the time. Since you rented the taxi, you were in business for yourself.

Driving a cab at that time must not be confused with driving one today. At that time, there were few cars and folks took cabs all over. Downtown and the suburbs were terribly busy on the weekends and folks were very generous at that time.

It was at this time that Julie was after me to get my GED and I did. Then she convinced me to take a mail-type course for accident investigation , which over some months I passed. Julie's words to me at that time was not great, congratulations, or wonderful. She smiled and said, "Not bad for a guy with a 7th-grade education."

I obtained a library card and a used Royal Portable Typewriter and taught myself to type and read at the same time whenever I had the time. This went on for a few years. Then my son David was born.

At that time, a few men came into our lives that would prove especially important to helping me support my family.

The first was a man named Abe. Now Abe was, in the daytime, a US Meat Inspector for the federal government. Abe was married but loved to gamble. So, he told his wife that he was driving a cab, which I understand she didn't care for. So, Abe would take out his cab, but never work. He just paid for the rental every day.

I was working as a taxi dispatcher. I worked only till eleven at night and then was home with my family. I also had another benefit since the owners of the company allowed me to type and study as long as I took care of business.

It seems that there was a slaughterhouse that Abe covered at nights. Now sometimes Mr. R (the owner of the slaughterhouse) would receive cows after hours from different states and sometimes broke their legs. Not all the time, but sometimes. I understand that the cow could not be slaughtered unless witnessed by a US inspector. Because of a rule about hours, these cows could not be used . It could only be used for other uses and if the possible value of the meat were in the hundreds, the broken leg and the lack of a US meat inspector brought the price down to really nothing.

Mr. R would call me looking for Abe. He wanted Abe to come and witness. I understand this, there is nothing illegal about this, because Abe was available and could put his seal on it.

Since they need him all the time, Abe gave me a telephone number where I could get him at any time.

Now, Mr. R had a policy that if anyone purchased meat from him, mostly copious amounts, and they didn't like it, then he would exchange it or give their money back. If this happened, Mr. R was not allowed to resell this meat and I was given many sides of beef.

I had to buy a freezer to hold all of it. Also, because of Mr. R's religion, there were things given to him by ranchers and farmers that he would accept but his religion would not allow . Like fresh scrapple. I checked with a lawyer friend of my dads who said it was legal .

So, our meat problem was taken care of. There were many times when we had too much, and we shared it with family and friends.

The second man was especially important to my family and to me in particular. His name was Michael.

We all, at some time in our lives, get to meet one or two special folks that come into our lives causally and have the power or ability to cause a small or major change in the direction of our lives. At the time, it was not realized by us and certainly unknown by them. Besides my parents and family, I was blessed with a few such people. The first, of course, was my wonderful wife, Julianne, then Abe and Michael, who is also a resident of heaven.

Admittedly, Julianne and I, after we married, had no idea or no plan of what the future had in store for us as we started our journey into married life and starting a family. We only knew we were in love and had each other.

Then I met Michael at work, before I married. He was just there, and to me now, it seems that it was planned for us to meet and be friends. Michael, along with my Julie, would make me see that there was a plan for me to be the father that I always dreamed of being. I wanted to be like the fathers of all the neighbor kids I grew up with during the Depression and World War II and admired and considered to be hero-like.

Michael always listened to me, asked questions, heard my stories about not being able to read or spell, my other disappointments, and small type failures that had occurred to me. Michael made me understand that disappointment and failures were sometimes good. The real thing was in the way you personally felt and just how you managed them. If you just gave up, then you were a failure. But if you reviewed each instance, saw the reason, and tried again, then you could never be a loser. As a father, you have accepted this obligation to be the captain of your family's ship. Failure, therefore, was not an option.

Now Michael was not a genius or a dummy. He was neither rich nor poor. He was a good friend and many times a big pain in the butt.

Michael was just an ordinary father and family man like me that just cared. He wanted nothing from me, he just wanted to give his advice and suggestions. He took time to teach me things I should have, but did not know at the time. He made me see, and then he helped Julianne and me to see that there were many possible roads ahead of us in life.

He cautioned us that there would be difficulties in our married lives, but we had to be strong and understand that together we could overcome almost anything. Which in real life we did.

Michael was also instrumental in helping Julianne and I obtain our first home when our son David was six months old. He was real estate salesman working for his brother, who was a broker. Michael convinced a seller to hold a private mortgage for us, with no down payment. Then he had his cousin, a lawyer, to manage the closing with no charge. Julie and I paid extraordinarily little to obtain our first house.

We would live in it for the next forty years and raise six children. We moved into the house, and we brought Julie's mother to live with us since her father had died. Eventually, there was nine people in a house with one bathroom. Julie's mother was a blessing to Julie because she knew that she was safe with us, and she helped Julie with the children.

It was a happy household, and we had many overnight visits from Sister Marie Pauline a catholic nun. She brought prayers, lessons, and rosary beads to our children.

There were two times that Mike called and wanted me to help him with something, but each time he said he had to go show someone a house. He asked me to go with him. I walked through the homes with the people and talked to them. After the showing, Mike always said he forgot he had to do something, and he would take me home.

Mike also drove a cab. I had a few folks from when I drove that liked me and would wait for me to take them home. One was a professor at Princeton University and the other at Trenton State Teacher's College. Both of these men told me over and over again that I did not belong as a taxi driver. Because I was now a dispatcher, I sent Mike a few times to take them home.

One night I was finishing work as the dispatcher when Mike called and wanted me to come to his brother's office. I was to bring four coffees. Which I did. When I arrived, I was surprised to see the two professors sitting there.

Mike quickly told me why. He said, "Do you remember me taking you on those two houses showing?"

"Yes," I said.

"Well," he said, "I have to tell you that both of those folks were mad at me because I had neglected them. If you remember, I never said a word. You did all the talking, pointing out things to them. Well, they both bought the houses." Then he showed me the check and said, "you are not going to get a dime of this. I am not even going to pay for the coffee; we three planned this to show you your ability. Now get a Real Estate License."

He was the one person who, along with my wife, made me continue my education and obtain my New Jersey Real Estate License. Unknowingly at the time, this started us on the path that made us successful and gave us, not a rich, but a comfortable and wonderful life.

We were friends for a few short years, laughed, worked, and traveled a lot.

Then one day Michael tragically died. For some reason, God took Michael from his family and friends. Julianne and I were devastated. We realized that we had a great friend in Michael. We then understood the effect he had on us, and we knew that we had to continue on the path Michael had so unselfishly helped us discover. Of course, Julianne and I have lived the life we chose, with God's help.

At the same time, I was selling Real Estate I started real estate appraising after being chosen by the Veterans Administration to be one of the appraisers. And I was still driving a taxi. It was safe and it was a wonderful experience to be a driver at this time. It all worked within my time. There were very few robberies and folks were making money and happy and used cabs a lot.

During this time, Julie and I were blessed once again with the births of another son and daughter, Edwin III and Linda Rose .

Julie, (God bless her) had her hands full with now five children: Shari, Michael, David, Eddie, and Linda. She had the help of her mother who lived with us. There were many times I felt bad not being there to help. Julie made me understand that I was doing all I could as a father and working toward better things for all of us.

THE CHRISTMAS PARTY:

My next story is to, once again, show and demonstrate the kindness of folks. It will clearly show how folks, working together for the benefit of others, were there for each other and stepped up to the plate when needed. Many times, without been asked.

This happened really spontaneously during a coffee break and a conversation with four guys: cab drivers, good friends, and fathers. They were Charlie, Wayne, Herman, and we were at a local hotel restaurant.

The hotel was located in the center of town and a married couple, Jimmy, and Laura, operated and managed the restaurant. (The hotel and restaurant are no longer there today.) This restaurant was a favorite place in downtown Trenton for all cab drivers, policemen, firemen, off duty waitresses, and many other folks that worked downtown

Charlie, Wayne, Herman, and I had a few things in common. We all were great friends, we all drove a taxi, and we all had children. It was in November (I forget what year), and we were talking about our kids. We were also talking about the fact that most businesses were having a Christmas party for the children of their employees.

We all knew that we were really in business for ourselves, and the Taxi Company was not going to have a Christmas party for our kids. At the time I was the President of the cab driver's Teamsters Union.

 Loving our kids, the way we all did, it just came out. It was Charlie's idea. "Why can't we have a Christmas party for our kids?" he said.

"Yeah," I said. He could ask Jimmy and Laura permission to use their hall. (Next to the restaurant they had a large meeting hall with a stage.)

We then talked for a while and all left to return to work, but we all agreed to return later that night for another coffee break. During this time, I guess all four of us were thinking of what we had talked about. When we returned to the restaurant, we were greeted by Jimmy and Laura, who had overheard us, and said that they would be more than happy for us to use their hall and stage for our Christmas party.

We going to have some type of Christmas party, even if only our kids come."

We started planning right there and then, none of us having any idea of what we were getting into.

We went home that night, told our wives, and enlisted their blessing and help. Julie loved the idea. Some other cab drivers voiced a desire to join in and have their kids included.

That night, the four of us all put in some money and decided that we were going to circulate a list for guys with kids that wanted to be included to sign and another list asking for contributions. As were we talking, two waitresses, off duty from another restaurant, overheard us and offered us money. They were not coming, but just wanted to help. They just thought it was a clever idea. The folks that frequent this restaurant, only plain working folks, were some of the finest people I ever met in my life.

I don't know just how, but the word got around, and we were making contributions. It was agreed that Charlie, Wayne, and me would be in charge of this. Charlie was the treasurer, but I am not sure.

There were many others that wanted to be part of this. Now please forgive me, as here I cannot mention any names, without their permission. But there were many.

I was surprised because contributions also came from other places. From costumers of Jimmy's restaurant, from Trenton police and firemen that we knew. Now keep in mind that none of these folks were planning to come, but they wanted to help.

My mind cannot remember the number of kids that were there . So again, forgive me.

Next, out of nowhere, we were offered by a woman, who owned a local dance studio, since we had a stage and dressing area, she offered to have the five or six groups of dance students perform for our party, free of charge. Then a local balloon guy offered his services. Jimmy and Laura agreed to supply and cook the food for us at cost.

(They had already let us have the hall free.) Wow!

I remember we compiled a list of toys to get and then one night Charlie, Wayne and I went to Two Guys Department store in Bordentown and proceeded to buy many toys for kids of all ages. While in this store shopping I ran into my Aunt Margaret, who after she heard what we were doing, gave me a great donation.

We bought many baskets of presents and wrapping paper. Our wives and friends helped wrap everything.

The party was held on a Saturday. We were ready. We had the food, hall, entertainment, and, of course, kids.

Jimmy and Laura and their crew put up a magnificent Christmas tree in the hall and decorated it for Santa to give out presents. However, we had no Santa.

So, we picked a guy no one would ever think of picking to play this jolly old man. He was a notoriously grumpy man; he was a paratrooper. His name was Carl. Carl had five children who were coming. Carl turned out to be the best Santa I ever saw.

Needless to say, the party was a smash. The dancers were outstanding, all six to twelve years of age. Tap dancing, beautiful costumes.

Jimmy and Laura and their crew cooked for all of us, the dancers, and their parents too.

This is a simple story of a bunch of daddies wanting to have a party for their children. I was proud to have been a part of this, as I know Charlie is too. Good old Wayne and Herman are both now with God, but they enjoyed it too. God Bless you guys.

This is just how it happened, and once again it shows and demonstrates in true fashion, not only the kindness of folks, but also through my words and memory, the way it truly was back then.

When someone had a tragedy or needed something, the folks I knew and grew up with were there. You didn't even need to ask.

A silly little party that four friends wanted to have, and you saw the results.

Speaking frankly, I was so proud that we were able to give my children, as well as all of the other children, one great Christmas. Julie loved being involved too.

I was happy being a cab driver; at that time we all we were important to the community. We played a role in a lot of people's lives. We took them to work, brought them home, and took grandma and granddad to the doctors, and countless other things. It was a business to all of us, not just a job. We were their cab drivers. There when they needed us.

These folks are all the hardworking, caring fool KS that looked out for us or served us "After hours and primary on weekends " in the 1950s, 1960s, and still today.

During the week, we worked all day in the bustling city and caring for our families, neighbors, and friends. Our kids were going to school, needed help with homework, and the various activities you had to go to for them. We all needed to relax.

Those after hours and those always so wonderful, welcomed, and so needed weekends. Oh, those weekends. They were really something we all looked forward to and remember even now. We just loved going out, to our favorite movie, bowling, dancing, tavern, restaurant, or dinner. These hours were to relax and enjoy with friends and families.

The folks that I would like to bring your attention and pay tribute was the many "Night Folks" that you might have forgotten.

The policeman, bartenders, waitresses, taxi drivers, dancers, singers, and entertainers of all kinds. Those women that worked in those Italian bakeries you stop at on the way home after work. The bagel makers on Second Street that you stopped off on Saturday nights to get bagels from to bring home.

Those night folks that were there waiting to help if needed. Many that you never saw, like ambulance drivers, nurses, doctors, firemen, cooks, bus drivers, and many more that I might have forgotten. There were thousands.

These were folks that help made your off hours safe, entertaining, pleasant, and delicious, and, yes, memorable.

These were our families, our relatives, our neighbors, some working second jobs. These folks were the night people that are also part of the history and the stories of our neighborhoods. They were there in all kinds of weather, very dependable, and just as important as the day folks like teachers, factory workers, state workers, and others.

TO GRANDMOM AND GRANDPOP'S HOUSE ON CHRISTMAS:

It had always been a ritual that the entire family would gather at my mother and fathers house on the holidays. Especially on Christmas. My mother, with the help of my sister Joyce, planned the next Christmas gathering the day after Christmas. They would plan and buy things all year round. My children would get up on Christmas morning, open their gifts, and after lunch were ready for their annual visit to their grandparent's house.

All the brothers and sisters and their families would be there, as it was year after year. Dad would be in the kitchen serving beer, Mom and Joyce would be running up and down the cellar stairs bringing fifty-gallon bags of toys and gifts to each child. It was always unbelievable what they spent and gave to each child. Mom and Dad said that this was their way of making up to their children all the toys and goodies that they were unable to give to us growing up. Even though we each told them that this was unnecessary, they still did it very year.

Mom always had something "extra" on the side. If there was a new boyfriend or girlfriend or unexpected visitor to her house, she had a gift for them. Dad would sing Christmas songs and cry because he remembered that as a child, he never had a family like he saw in front of him.

This event happened year after year, and I can tell you that on occasion, my children have told me that this memory of Christmas with Grandma and Granddad will live in their minds and hearts forever.

This same thing would happen again at Easter. Mom loved to have all the kids there, although the neighbors were not happy with us taking their parking spots.

PRECIOUS MOMENTS I REMEMBER:

This reminds me of something else, something sealed in my mind and very precious to me that I also would like to share.

During all this time, Julie and I were blessed with the births of Edwin III, Linda Rose, and Sandra. Julie and I were happy, even thought it was not always easy. We had six wonderful children. But take into consideration we lived through good times, lean times, and tough times.

When I slept, I slept on my right side, with my back to Julie. It really happened for the first time long before, right after Shari was born. Early in the morning, I awoke to feel Julie using her finger as a pencil. She was writing something on my back. She thought that I was asleep. I asked her what she wrote. She said, "I wrote 'I love you.' "

I could not get over that, she was lying in bed thinking that I was sound asleep, she woke, and wrote that. She knew I slept well. Many times, after that, I felt her writing, but I never let her know that I was awake.

As I said before, Julie was, behind our bedroom doors and other places we were alone, very affectionate and she was a hand holder. In the early years, in the older car, in those days, she sat close to me. She would reach out for my hand when we walked, in the movies, and sat watching TV. We held hands watching her favorite TV show,

We, like all married folks, had our small arguments and disagreements, but at night, with our bedroom door closed, we worked things out over and over again. Behind those doors, Julie kept up the steady pace of keeping up my confidence. She kept telling me that I could do anything I wanted. I told her that because I was working two jobs and studying, I was neglecting her and the kids. So, we made a habit of talking every Sunday and doing something together. We drove to the Seaside, maleficent , mountains, to Lancaster, Valley Forge, and to Edison's Museum. In addition, we went on picnics and every fast-food place around at that time.

Then we started, for the first time, considering going away with the whole gang on vacation. I was in real estate and in March I sold my first house and got a considerable commission. So, we planned to go to a place Julie found called Vacation Valley Lounge in the Pocono's.

At the time, I had made friends with many folks, attorneys, Realtors, and wealthy men. They all knew that I had a big family and they all offered me their different vacation homes in the mountains and at the shore. I thanked them. However, I was aware that if we did use their place and something happened to their property, it would have a lasting effect on our relationship.

 The biggest reason I had, and told Julie, was that if we did use someone's house, we would have to buy food, cook, and clean. In my mind that would not be a vacation for her. I did not want that for her. She deserved to be waited on like any other person on vacation and to enjoy herself while we were there.We then tried to go away each year.

I remember that each Sunday, like during football season, we would find a field and throw the football. Then we would go to some dinner. Do you have any idea what it costs to feed eight people lunch? As a family, we made trips to the boardwalk in Seaside, to the puddle boats in Washington Crossing, Philly's baseball games, and to many parks just to throw around the football. Then Vacation Valley Resort and Lake Wallenpaupack in the Pocono's or riding to the top of Mount Pocono. We took many day trips in all kinds of weather. Many times, we would try to include one of our kid's friends., We took my mom and dad there once.

My children loved a man there named Jewal. He was the entertainment director of the resort, and also a dog they called Sam. Jewal would have things for the kids to do swimming, horseback riding, hat rides, and things like that. Each of the resorts had a huge alpine dining room, where each family had a table, and we could come and go when eating breakfast. On each Saturday, they had a Hawaiian Luau, complete with Hawaiian girls putting lei around each person's neck. They had roast pig and all the traditional trimmings. It was great.

We tried to make up to our children for working hard and not always having the time for them.

JULIE AND SAINT FRANCIS HOSPTIAL:

It was at this time Julie and I would go to dinner with friends, and we enjoyed that. Julie's childhood friend also had six children and had moved right down the street from us, Ae were always in each other's house or our kids were in each other's house. At one of these dinners, Ada told us that she had taken a part-time job at Saint Francis Hospital. Four hours at night delivering food to the rooms. The hospital was a few blocks from our house.

After we got home, I suggested to Julie that she also apply for a job. Now she has not worked in years and was a housewife and mother. But that was the problem. I realized that for all these years, even though her mother lived with us, that all she did all day was talk to children and I thought she needed a change. Her mother could take care of the family while she worked.

Unbeknownst to me at the time, but I was right. After she got the job, Julie changed a little; she seemed a little happier. It seems that another friend who lived nearby and also grew up with Julie and Ada, Jan, also got a job there. She had seven children. They would go to work and be on the phone all night talking about their supervisor or what happened that day. While it was true that the money helped, it was more important to me that she took this break, it was long overdue.

Julie, Ada, and Jan had these jobs for about two years.

At this time, I was studying and working, and life was good.

Then for some reason, I noticed that Julie was not feeling too good. I just felt it, but she of course said that she was all right. Then one day we had to rush her to Strains, and we found out that she was having an appendicitis attack. So, they had to suddenly operate on her. When I visited her, Julie was in a lot of pain after the operation. I stayed with her for hours, but then went home to check on the children and her mother. I slept on the couch for a while then was on my way back to see her when I had another heart attack and was once again in CCU. Julie was on the third floor, and I ended up in CCU. It was because all that time, while sitting with her and when I went home, I was feeling her pain.

Julie was not happy, and it was not explainable now I had this attack. It was because we loved each other and were so close. You might not understand that, but I think that's what it was.

Julie would have to heal for months; however, I had sprung back and was back to my duties. Julie was back at home was a great mother helping the kids deal with her recovery. Once again, we started to go out at times to various places to be alone together.

On some Sundays, we would get my mother and take her for long rides. Both Julie and my mother loved to drive in Pennsylvania. As we drove around, Mom would remember both good things and sad things about her childhood. One of these things she never seemed to get over was that after her mother died, her brothers and sisters were all gathered together. There was a genuinely nice lady that told them that they would be taken to loving farmers that longed for children and could not have them. These were good homes, and the people would take diligent care of them. They were also told that they would all get back together at some time. But mom said it was a lie. They all were taken to various places and never heard from again. She was forced to live with her grandfather, who had a housekeeper that hated mom and made her life miserable.

THE REUNION:

My mother wanted badly to find her brothers and sisters. It had been almost sixty years since she saw them. We found out that one of her older sisters, Lillian, might be nearby.

 Once again, Mom was born in Norristown, Pa, in 1910. Her mother had been widowed and she had three children. Her first husband was named Corcoran, who's nephew was Mickey Corcoran, the great Major League baseball player. Then she married my mother's father and had five other children before she was thirty-three years of age. Then my grandmother died at the age of thirty-six years old. It seems that my mom's dad could not work, and all the kids were separated. My mom was twelve at the time.

The family, for some reason or other, could not find each other. Authorities would not help with records and my mom wanted so badly to find one of them. I had a particularly good friend who was a police dispatcher that moved to Pennsylvania. He lived in one of those small county communities. It was one of five towns that used the same police force and emergency services.

He knew a lot about my mother's missing sister because I told him. His family was also looking for their lost relatives. He called me one day and told me that he had found my Aunt Lillian, who was living in a small town near him. We compared notes and thought we had a match. I would have to go there to see for sure.

One Sunday, Julie and I took Mom for a ride, which we did a lot since she loved to ride in the country. Our plan was to ride up there and I was to get out and see if this lady was my mother's sister. At the time I thought she was not Lillian but didn't know. So, we told mom I had to check something, and it might be a long ride. When we arrived, I got out of the car, found the house, and rang the bell. The lady answered and she was not my mom's lost sister.

So, I asked, "Do you know Emma Cole?"

To that, her eyes grew large and almost instantly started to tear. "Oh, oh, God, that's my sister whom I have not seen in over sixty years"

I had not really planned this; I really thought this ride was a waste of time.

But it was true. God, now how can I go tell my mom that we found her sister? She was unprepared and I was afraid she might have a heart attack. But I could not stop now. I then told Lillian that she's outside in my car right now. She rushed to my car; my mother was looking at her with her mouth open. She did not recognize Lillian, so I opened the door, held mom tightly, and slowly told her that this was her long-lost sister. God was that a night. They cried; they held each other out there in the cold.

Julie and I made them go inside. The crying and hugging and the thanking to God went on for about twenty minutes.

 Long after, Julie and I said to each other that there could be no other act in the world that could top the feeling we both had, for not only finding Lillian, but having the extreme pleasure of watching it all. To my mom and Lillian, at the time of that meeting, in their minds Julie and I were not even there. What a feeling.

We took pictures of it all.

Lillian, before the night was over, let Mom know about her brother Joseph, that she had also not seen in sixty years, lived in Pennsylvania not far from here. Lillian said they tried to find her, but records were not allowed to be seen in those days. (We would go the next week to see her brother Joe and Julie and I got to witness another reunion). We then found out that Joe had the family Bible.

My mom cried repeatedly on the way home, she didn't want to leave and thanked us a million times before we reached home.

 A SURPRISED GET A WAY:

One summer Friday night, I went to work early, about 2:30 in the afternoon. When I arrived, there was a friend of mine, Richie, who was completely devastated. He had been separated from his wife for years, had two grown sons, and was trying over and over again to reconcile with his wife for years. He explained that he planned and paid for a weekend in a honeymoon resort in the Pocono's for this weekend and that she refused him. He then told me that he could not get his money back since it was too late and offered it to me.

I called Julie and told her. I asked her to try to get someone to help her mother, so that I could get someone to replace me so that we could use these reservations. Julie loved the idea and sometime later we were on our way for a great and wonderful weekend.

The place was named Apple Resort. When you entered, there was red carpeting and clear glass tables with apples on each table. A round bed with mirrors on the ceiling and a private pool with sauna. Our meals were delivered.

This was wonderful and it was the Hollywood we never had or could afford. As a result, as expected, our third daughter was conceived.

Julie then made sure that I went to see the doctor to prevent any more children. We lovingly refer to Sandy at times as our "Mountain Baby."

LEARNING CONTINUES ON:

During all of these times, I was trying daily to better myself. I was now a Real

Estate Salesman and an appraiser. I was slowly getting more into the Real Estate and appraisal fields with Julie's help.

I had taught myself how to read and spell better and was still learning. I soon discovered that I really understood the act of evaluating property. It was true that I never worked in construction or the other building occupations; however, I learned amazingly fast, and it seemed easy for me to comprehend things fast.

Also, at this time, I learned that I could explain things to others and soon I was called to speak at chapter meetings throughout the state. So, Julie and I traveled and met a lot of new, wonderful folks.

It would turn out long after this period of time was the best time to enter the appraisal field. In the 1960s, there was no licensing or requirements for appraising except with the Appraisal Institute, which really just manage commercial property. In addition, there were no mortgages as we know them today. There were Building & Loans, Saving & Loans, and banks.

At this time, anyone with a business and a letterhead could, and did, call themselves appraisers. Lawyers and folks would hire them, and they would just give a letter-typed opinion.

The Building & Loans, Savings & Loans, and bank used something different. The mortgage officers, along with members of the boards, would just ride up, look at the exterior, and decide how much they thought the property was worth and how much to loan. That became known as a "ride-by appraisal."

Also, at this time, the Multiple Listings System of the Board of Realtors was really in its infancy. The system they used at that time was listing a property, the board trying a picture, and making a poster-type page on a single letter-size paper, poking three holes in it, and sending it to the Realtors every two weeks, which then they placed in a three-prong binder. All updates and new listings were sent that way. It was called an activity sheet, were the realtors had to update, mostly with pen or pencil, things like price changes, sales dates, and selling prices. This is something that not all Realtors did. Therefore, a lot of the data in their offices was old and often incorrect.

I was invited to join a new organization known as the National Association of Independent Fee Appraisers out of Saint Louis. It offered all types of education that I needed.

I seemed to click with the new appraisers I met and started to learn increasingly about the appraisal business. I was already on the VA list and then got on to the FHA list.

I then took many courses and found that I loved this business.

Soon, I was elected to become a chapter officer and worked my way up to chapter president. Within two years I was elected and became New Jersey State Director for two years. As state director, I had to attend the National Meetings all over the country. Many times, Julie came with me. This was funded by the chapter.

For the Veterans Administration, I covered the counties of Mercer, Burlington, Camden, Ocean, Atlantic, and Cape May. I had to go to these counties to appraise homes. When I did, I needed to stop at some Realtors Office and obtain closed sales in each area. This was exceedingly difficult, because many times the realtors would not let you use their data or wanted to charge you. And if you did get the activity sheets, the data on the sheets, in many cases, was not updated or correct.

Then at one of the IFA meetings, I was given a list of appraisers that were also realtors that belonged to our organization and were willing to share and help you if you stopped by. I copied the complete list during that meeting.

After that I also offered my data and help to all of the other members. Soon I was stopping by in all those counties and I got to meet all the appraisers. There were times when they would stop what they were doing to help me. I felt bad that I was taking them from their work and offered to pay them or take them to lunch. But they refused, just saying they were glad to help.

It just happened that I, as state director, was sent by the chapter to the National Convention in Pittsburg. It was there that I was asked to be on the Public Relations Committee and was chosen at that first meeting to be the chairman.

The purpose of the committee was to produce ideas for requirements and to promote our organization. That meant now, after I returned home, I had to go to many chapter meetings in NJ, PA, and NY to promote our organization, our educational courses, and recruit members.

Julie went with me and each time I spoke, I would come back to our table and asked her, "How did that sound?" Or "Was I all right?" She always told me I was good.

At the next National Board of Directors Meeting, as I was making my report, I suggested to the board that they consider my recommendation that we refer to our organization hereafter with a brand-new motto, which was:

" NAIFA: THE SHARING AND CARING ORGANIZATION"

I explained about when I joined this group and the difficulties that I and all members had getting correct data from Realtors. How it was my personal experience that our members were always there, available with the correct data. To me, that was a notable example of caring and sharing. Of course, they agreed.

CONGRESS:

As I told you before, in the early years there was no requirement, education, or any type of control on folks giving out housing values. So, a few of the officers of the nine original appraisal organizations got together. We held a meeting, and all decided that we would like to get congress to make it a law and that there should be experience and education requirements for the people giving values of the public's greatest assets. At the same time, we realized that we also would have to get each state to adopt whatever congress would approve.

So, we found Congressman Bernard of South Carolina and he drafted the first bill that went to congress. We then lobbied and arranged busloads of appraisers to go to Capitol Hill and see the representatives and convince them. At the same time, we were doing the same thing in our states. We had to testify in both places. We had to collaborate closely with some committees educating them on our business and suggesting what educational and experience requirements we thought was fair and practical. We suggested three designations with three distinct levels. They were Licensed Appraiser, Certified Appraiser, and General Appraiser.

Well it took time, but it passed through congress and the states and became law. Then tests needed to be taken for each level. The education testing corporation out of Princeton, NJ, was selected to draft and oversee these tests. Since they knew nothing about our business, they required questions from us to ask on these tests. I was on that committee.

I AM ESPECIALLY PROUD OF THESE TWO
THINGS THAT BECAME PART OF THE
INDUSTRY

THE FOLKS THAT OFFERED THEIR TIME
IN MAKING OUR BUSINESS WHAT IS
TODAY WERE MY FRIENDS AND
EXCEPTIONAL PEOPLE.

WE ARE ALL REFERED TO AS THE
"PIONEERS OF THE APPRAISAL
INDUSTRY." I LOVE BEING CALLED THAT.

ALSO, I CLAIM CREDIT FOR GIVING THE
NAIFA THE "CARING AND SHARING
ORGANIZATION" SLOGAN: Because
after our organization approved my
slogan, it was then known to the entire
housing, lending, government agencies,
banks, savings and loans, and the world.
It has been spoken in hundreds of
speeches, thousands of news releases

As National Public Relations Chairman
for nine years, and also as National
Director of the NAIFA, I represented our
organization at many National

Association of Realtor's Conventions manning a booth in New Orleans; Las Vegas; Honolulu, HI; Miami Beach, FL; Anaheim, CA; and Atlanta, GA.

It was during this time, I met a man that lived in Cape May, NJ. He was a deacon in a church, but also an appraiser and he asked me to be part of that year's Marine's Toys for Tots program. I agreed. It happened that we had an educational course at one of the casinos in Atlantic City, NJ. This man came to me and told me that after class he wanted to have a small meeting with other folks who were volunteering in this matter. So, after class, we walked into a lounge and there sitting next to each other were Al Alberts and his wife Stella.

Now Al was my hero. An idol to many, a great singer, and had a TV show on Channel 6 in Philadelphia for thirty years. Ever since I was in my teens, I had been a fan of Al Alberts and the Four

Aces. I had bought and sung his songs over and over again. Al had won two Academy Awards in Hollywood in the past for best song in a motion picture. One was for "Love Is a Many Splendor Thing," and the other was from the picture "Three Coins in a Fountain."

I could not believe they asked me to sit next to them and offered me a drink. I would, along with Julie, become friends with them for the rest of our lives. Al and Stella both liked me. We did Toys for Tots together and we stayed in touch. Al knew that I could write lyrics and wanted me to get back into it. He and Stella liked the few I showed them. I had a habit of ending all my letters with: "Smile—Ed." Folks started to refer to me as "Smiley."

Soon, at the National Conventions, I became friends with people from all parts of the United States of America. Julie and my mother went with me to

Cleveland, West Virginia, New York, Denver, Nashville, and other places.

My daughter Linda had an illness (which I will discuss later in the book), and this caused Julie to stop traveling with me to stay home with her.

Wherever I went, I knew that Julie was there with me. Silently cheering me on. I was trying desperately to juggle working, serving as an officer, and being home at the same time. Julie said she wanted me to keep going.

No matter what, we had Sunday's reserved as family day. Many times, we went places, other times it was just out to eat. We tried to juggle that one week it was a fast-food place, the next week a dinner, and many times in a hotel restaurant.

Some weekends we stayed in for the football games. I loved the Cowboys,

Julie was a Redskins Fan, Mike was an Oakland fan, and Shari and Dave were Vikings Fans. Needless to say, there were many boo's and celebrations in our living room week after week. Julie and I instructed our kids about football and country music when they were young. Julie and I bought many records of children's music and songs. both of us believed that music was so important and vital to children. A few of our children today have musical instruments and sing in a band.

HEART ATTACK:

I am now involved in the real estate business. I was selected to be in charge of the hospitality room at the State Realtors Convention in Atlantic City, NJ. It was held at, then known as Haddon Hall, which later became Resorts Casino.

I was driving home after the convention when I was suddenly soaked with sweat. When I reached home, I was extremely sick. A neighbor took me to

Saint Francis Hospital. I was knocked out and we discovered that I had had a heart attack. I don't remember much. I was so tired; I slept a lot. I woke found myself in CCU ward, with needles and tubes in me. I had a great, pulsing headache from the drugs they were putting in me to keep my veins open.

Then I saw the face of my bride, who looked scared. She sat down and held my hand and with tears in her eyes, said, "Eddie, don't leave me." I remember her look and those words so well. Seeing her so upset, I started to joke, telling her there was nothing wrong with me. She made me promise to slow down and take care of myself.

I was told that this would leave a scar. When they checked, they said that there were scars on my heart that indicated that twice before I had apparently had two minor attacks and that I was to take it easy for a while. Which I did. This was the first time in my life as an adult that I ever collected unemployment and would be the only time.

CENTURY21 MACNICOLL AGENCY:

I had obtained my broker's license and opened an office in our living room, after having a box windows and the room converted into an office. But that did not work out. I then became office manager for two realtors. Each time I did something new, Julie did not tell me, good, great, congratulations, she would say her usual, "Not bad for a guy with a 7th-grade education."

You have no idea of just how many times I wanted to stop. That I could not study, that I was just too tired, and many times just overwhelmed with trying.

There were so many times during those years that I felt inadequate and discouraged. But Julie would close our bedroom door and work her magic. She made me feel and understand that I could do whatever I wanted. Even though at the time where we were heading , she told me that she would be there with me all the way. For me not to worry about her and the kids or the house. She would do that. She wanted me to continue to whatever levels I wanted.

It was about 1979. A lawyer friend of mine, who was a judge, called and had dinner with me. He offered to fund me and become my partner. He gave me the money to buy a Century21 franchise.

Soon, I was in California attending a week-long school for new Century21 franchise owners. There I met folks from all over the United States of America. My mind soaked in all the education I could. I was incredibly happy and totally impressed with the quality of the education that was and would be available to me and my future sales staff.

After I returned, we opened an office down the street from the judge. I then hired a total of forty-three salespersons. Three of them were brokers that once had their own officers but closed, including the realtor that I originally started in the real estate business with. Some of them brought their existing staff.

Things and our future looked good. Julie was my treasurer and my daughter Shari worked answering the phone.

I had even started my very own newspaper and went out and solicited popular spots where I could distribute them.

My father was immensely proud, and he read my ads in the newspaper each and every day. He would spot mistakes and let me know, as I got a credit or reduction for the mistake.

Then things got bad. The mortgage interest rate went to 20 percent. No one was buying. It was true we had many sellers, but no one could get a mortgage because of the new requirements and high interest rate.

For months we tried to hold on, but my reserves were getting low. Reluctantly I had to decide. The judge did not want to provide so I talked to Julie, and we chose to close. But if I did close, I would be breaking leases and maybe would have to declare bankruptcy. S

o, I found a broker who agreed to take over all my obligations and keep my sales staff and everything intact. However, he did not want the franchise, so I sold that to another realtor, and we ended my dream. I was so upset, frustrated, and sad. I had worked so hard, and I did everything right and none of this was my fault but the fault of the country.

As a result, I had another heart attack. This time I had struts put into my veins at Our Lady of Lords in Camden, NJ.

This is when Julie and I took a drive to the New Jersey Shore, and I have no shame in telling you I cried like a baby. Then I told Julie that I liked appraising homes and that I was good at it. I had been thinking now for weeks and I knew that this is what I wanted to do for the rest of my life. I remember just what I said. "Julie, in real estate appraising, as compared to owning my own Real Estate office, we might never be rich, but we will have a comfortable life"

APPRAISAL EXCHANGE, INC:

After I recovered, I rented an office in Hamilton Township and opened my appraisal office. The judge helped me become an incorporate and the name was Appraisal Exchange, Inc. Once again, my Julie was there as office manager and treasurer. We hired about nine appraisers at the time, (There was no licensing requirements for appraisers at these time) three women to type the reports, and we were in business.

At times we had more business then we could manage. Julie also started to appraise. I loved it because she would collaborate with a woman that was with us at the Real Estate Office, and they were friends. They would do the appraisals and then go to lunch or shopping or hang out. This was good for Julie.

Then something happened: I was one of the first professionals that purchased a fax machine in this area. Because of this, I started to get faxed appraisal requests. This increased my business. It was at this time; I personally trained many appraisers that left us and went to work for themselves.

Julie was so mad at me. She told me, and of course she was right, that I was training my competition. So, I stopped.

Then I started to get appraisal assignments in Cape May, Atlantic, and Ocean counties. It was wonderful. We had kids in two different schools then, so I would plan to appraise appointments in the late mornings and Julie, sometimes my mother, and any child who was home that day, we all would take a ride. They would wait in the car and then we would stop for lunch someplace. Mom and Julie loved it. Two of our favorites were the Forked River House that has an alpine interior with a huge fireplace that was warm and cozy in the winter and then there was The Captain's Inn on the water for the summer. We always seemed to make it home in time to be there for our children. Those were wonderful times.

During this period, I made a lot of money and life was good.

When I had assignments in Cape May or Atlantic county, and since my Julie and my mother were slot machine lovers, I would take them to a casino, do my work, and then pick them back up on the way home.

I remember the buckets of quarters they both brought home and kept until the next visit.

GETTING MY SONTO JOIN ME.

It was also at this time that I convinced my son David to become a full-time appraiser. He was working for the State of New Jersey delivering things all over the State. David hated the traffic. One day, I said to him, "How much does the State pay you?" He told me and I agreed to pay him that amount if he came with me and learned how to appraise, even if he only came with me one day a week.

That is how David entered this business. Sitting in the passenger seat of my car was like sitting in a classroom because I never shut up. Although unsure, very timid, and shy, David went on to be a great appraiser and is one of the only men I have ever meet that, like I, absolutely loves what he does for a living.

My son Michael was our night man. He loved working at night alone. He played all the records we had and more. He was particularly good at what he did and in return he made a great living. Michael was there once again for Julie and me when we were away. Holding down the fort, managing messages, and watching our office at all times.

Our youngest son Eddie also learned early on to appraise but was still pursuing an education. He was except into the College of New Jersey, and we worked to help him. He then went into the prescription drug industry as a chief Pharmaceutical Programmer and is very respected in his field.

Our oldest daughter Shari also worked in our office when she was young but was interested in other fields. She then married and started her own life. Julie also employed our daughters Linda and Sandy in the task of bookwork and accounting.

MY INTRODUCTION TO HISTORIC APPRAISING:

At the time I opened my appraisal office, throughout the country there was no licensing of appraisers. In most areas, it was typical for lawyers or whoever to hire real estate salespersons, builders, contractors, and others to express a value on their letterhead. These were all untrained folks .

The Veterans Administration and the Federal Housing Authority (FHA) were the only ones testing and approving fee appraisers. I happened to be one of those.

As I said before, although I had never been trained, I understand the act of value. I was always intrigued with the craftsmanship of our forefathers. In churches and in housing. I was once told by an old builder about the two prime periods in the history of housing. One was the Colonial period, and the other was the Victorian period.

The reason he taught me about all of this was because I helped him install a tub in a house. He explained that these were the only two types of housing in the United States of America. During the war, there was really nothing manufactured for the consumer, everything was made for the war effort. Therefore, if someone needed a heater, tub, sink, or anything for their homes, it was hard to find. So, folks would take these items out of old abandoned homes and make them fit.

There were many beautiful, vacant, and abandoned historical homes in our area. Because of all the new construction that sprang up after the war, folks were more interested in the new. Therefore, many of these architectural treasures, with handmade moldings, lay rotting. The only buildings that were being taken care of were ones that interested folks wanted to preserve. Most of those patrons were wealthy.

It happened that I was having lunch with a baker at the Washington Crossing Inn in Washington Crossing, PA. He pointed out a beautiful Federal -type house that was down the road and said that the owner wanted a loan. but could not find an appraiser that could place a reasonable value on it.

I told him that I thought I could. However, there was no guide for me to follow or form for a building of that type. So, I tried doing it, mainly because it was a challenge to me, and I had a love for historic, older homes.

To make a long story short, I developed my own form and completed the report. It was not the exact report they would have liked, but they accepted it anyway.

Soon I was in demand. As a result, the mayor of Trenton invited me to serve on the Trenton Landmarks Commission as a commissioner. I soon became chairman.

At this time, I was also elected in a national election to the Board of Directors of the National Association of Independent Fee Appraisers out of Saint Louis.

BUYING OUR OFFICES ON SOUTH BROAD STREET:

It was at this time that I purchased our office building on S Broad Street, which would be our home for the next twenty-five years. We had no other employees other than our family.

This office proved to be the greatest purchase Julie and I ever made. In the coming years, each and every one of our children will work for us. We, as a family, were so close-knit. It was true that our children, during this time, moved out on their own and some married. But each and every day for the next twenty or twenty-five years, they were with each other in this building every single day. They all taught and learned from each other.

We were located in an area where many folks walked by or visited us on a daily basis. We became friends with many of the neighbors. Realtors, salespersons, bankers, and other appraisers would stop by daily once or twice to say hello or visit with all of us. We had a few wonderful characters that my children will remember for the rest of their lives.

One was "Joe the Whip," an older man that totally adored Julie and my children. Then there was John, who was one of only three remaining survivors of the Pearl Harbor Attack in Hawaii of December 7, 1941.? The last was a retired Prison Guard that lived next door and his name was George. These three men were constantly in our offices, checking on us and helping us in any way they could. In this office, because I loved music, over the years I have collected hundreds and hundreds of records, tapes, and CDs of every type of music that one could imagine. Dave and Michael played them over and over again. I introduced both of them to music from the 1930s, 1940s, and 1950s.

They both played guitars and never had a single lesson.

That started a recital that started in our home when Dave and Mike were in their teens. They, with a few friends, would come to our house every Saturday and play and sing. These continued when Mike bought his own house, and it still continues to this day.

Some of them have since moved out of town. But no matter the weather, they all still meet. David and a few friends formed a band and played at many establishments in this area for years.

I know that Julie loved their visits. You could see that in her eyes and mannerism. As I predicted years before, we all made a very comfortable living and life was so good for all of us during those twenty years.

Today, I am immensely proud of my two sons, Michael, and David, who worked side-by-side with me and Julie for the next twenty years. They were both particularly good and respected Real Estate Appraisers. Without their constant help and just being there in our offices gave Julie and me the freedom to travel. After a while it gave me the freedom to travel, teach, and become the man I am.

I cannot really express my appreciation. Without Julie and my sons Michaels and

David's help, a lot of what I accomplished would have never happen. Few parents have the pleasure of living and working with their children as Julie and I had. I was so proud when bankers, lenders, and customers told me just how good and talented our sons were.

Our life during this time was so wonderful.

LINDA:

Our Daughter Linda, while attending Mercer Community College, developed a sickness known as "Agoraphobia." This causes the person to fear places that are unknown to them, appear vastly open, or dangerous to them. This fear often house-bounds most of them. It is said there really is no known cure. It has been known that in time, with many sufferings of this sickness, that one day it just disappears by itself.

Loving Linda as she did, Julie stayed with her and collaborated with her and her doctors. Of course, if Julie went away overnight, this would cause Linda to panic and become uneasy. So, Julie chose to stay home and not travel with me. I felt guilty and told Julie that I would stop and resign my offices. But Julie took me into our bedroom, closed the door, and once again worked her magic. She wanted me to continue in my climbing and my education. She once again told me that she would take care of the home front. She wanted and needed me to support our family as I was.

I cannot really express the devotion that my bride had for our daughter. Linda is and always has been a gentle, loving girl. Julie managed, over a period of time, to get Linda to slowly, day–by-day leave the house. Soon she got Linda to get into her car and started to drive slowly around the neighborhood. At first Linda resisted, but Julie kept it up.

Little by little, very day, they would drive. Julie enlisted the help of our youngest daughter Sandy and together, religiously every single day, regardless of the weather, they made their ride. The area Linda felt comfortable in grew and grew; to a point that now they were going shopping, having lunch, and coming to our office. They made bank deposits and regular trips to the post office.

Julie was a saint. Her love for our children was indescribable. This single, daily task the three of them did lasted over twenty years.

By this time, over the past twenty years, I have traveled on behalf of the National Association of Independent Fee Appraisers, The National Trust for Historic Preservation, as an officers, speaker, or national instructor all over the United States of America, Canada, and Mexico. I had been in very stated with the exception of the Northwest

States. I was in Montréal, Quebec, and Vancouver, British Columbia.

Each city I went to, I had to bring home three items. A timbale for Julie, a cookbook for Sandy, and a local book of strange events of the town for Linda .

MEETING CELEBRITIES :

I was in Phoenix, AZ, at the Camelback Resort at a convention. After the meeting, they were giving us a steak cookout on top of Mummy Mountain. My friends and I were walking up this steep road going to the top. It was extremely hot and humid. As we were walking, a man came by going up the mountain on a golf cart. He smiled at me, and I suddenly had an idea. I started to fake a limp. I stopped him and asked him if I could ride with him since I had a bad leg. He smiled and said sure, so up the mountain we went. My friends were shouting at me.

At the top of the mountain, there were large cooking stations, with many folks cooking steaks on an open fire. There were many buffet tables and tables to sit. There were two long lines of folks standing, moving up slowly to get their steaks hot off the fire. I got in one of these lines. Behind me was a gentleman and we talked.

Then my friends reached the top of the mountain, spotted me, and came up to me to razz me. The man, seeing that we were friends, turned to folks behind him and ask them if they mind if these guys butted in line to be with me. No, they said, and my friends joined us. I stayed with the man.

After we got our sizzling steaks, we looked for a table. The man said, they're all full. One of the guys spotted a table that folks were just about to leave. I invited him to hang with us and he did.

He was a genuinely nice man and he fit in with us crazy guys. He asked a lot of questions, like where you all come from and why are you here in Phoenix. Apparently, he lived here. Then I asked him the same questions and that's when we discovered that we were sitting on top of this mountain with a famous astronaut.

His name was Ronald Ellwin Evans Jr., and he was a NASA astronaut. He was one of only twenty-four people to have flown to the moon. He also served as a captain in the United States Navy.

He told us how he was selected as an astronaut by NASA as part of Astronaut Group 5 in 1966. He made his first and only flight into space as the command module pilot aboard Apollo 17 in 1972, the last manned mission to the moon to date, with Commander Eugene Cernan and Lunar Module Pilot Harrison Schmitt. During the flight, he orbited the moon as his two crew mates descended to the surface. At that time, he was the last person to orbit the moon alone. In 1975, Evans served as backup command module pilot for the Apollo-Soyuz Test Project mission.

We were fascinated with him as he explained as much as he could about how the earth looked and his adventures. I asked him what occupied him during his orbit around the moon and he said he had so much to do. He didn't have time to think and that the time went by fast. He talked about his training and the other astronauts that were his friends. We wanted to spend more time with him; however, a woman came and found him and said he had another engagement that night. He took our cards, gave all of us his, and said that he would send us a packet of him and his wife. He did a week later, and my son Edwin III has it somewhere.

It was an honor, and I often wonder how many people in this life get to meet a real hero like this. It was a simple, innocent, chance meeting on top of Mummy Mountain.

 LAS VEGAS 2000:

In 2000, all of the world's appraisal organizations agreed to meet for the first time in Las Vegas at the MGM Grand. It was commented that it would be a spectacular meeting and a chance for all real estate appraisers to meet, learn, exchange notes, and become friends.

In setting up the program, the committee wanted to offer some type of educational programs for the attendees. Since all organizations had required similar designation education for both residential and business classes, these would not be necessary. Therefore, they wanted specialized courses that might draw the interest of many.

My historic course was considered, and I had to reduce the course from two days to one day, which I did. My co-instructor, John, and I arrived the day before. Because of space limitation, the enrollment was set to eighty people. Since it was an elective, the class was sold out five days after it was offered.

The attendees were from forty different countries, including England, Holland, Ireland, Russia, Poland, Germany, France, Canada, Mexico, and other countries. The topic was based on the valuing of older, historic homes and buildings. It was meant to mainly draw interest to our organization. We were offering education to the members to learn about these properties in their own countries. We mainly utilized and explored the United States Colonial period and the Victorian period.

This was a great class and was given to a world stage. It was one of the proudest moments in my life as far as teaching was concerned, especially since I was the originator and the author of this course.

I had taken this from a simple idea to an approved course for educational credits, accepted by all the organizations and all the states.

John and I were given a standing ovation at the completion of the class.

ABOUT FAMILY: THE FINAL RESTING PLACE

It was during these years that we lost my father first, then years later my mother. But Mom had one other lasting gift to give her family.

As I explained before, my mother and father really never had what could be considered a real family. They tried all their lives to make all of their children feel and understand the meaning of families in everything that they did, such as the Christmas and Easters I described in this story.

I would like to point out that the following act is the greatest tribute to family that I have ever seen. I have never heard of anyone doing what I am going to tell you. Honestly, I, myself, would have never thought of it.

Mom knew that my dad loved the chimes of the church at Ewing cemetery. When he died, Mom, with Joyce's help, purchased his grave near the church. At the same time, they purchased a grave for both mom and Joyce. They also purchased a ceremonial grave for my oldest sister Thelma.

Then Mom suggested to Joyce that it would be nice if all of our family could be next to each other in this cemetery. They soon discovered that there were open lots right next to them. So, Joyce and Mom put a down payment on a total of fifty-nine graves sites. Each site could be used as two graves. This totaled a possible 114 grave sites next to them.

All the family could be together. This was a wish my mother wanted so badly. After Mom passed, my sister Joyce finished her dream by paying for them with her retirement money from General Motors.

Joyce then distributed them according to the size of each family. My bride Julie is buried there today. Joyce also fulfilled my mother's wish for my sister Patricia, who lived in Chicago, and purchased graves sites around Patricia's husband's grave for their family.

This, my friends, is my wonderful parent's and our oldest sister, Joyce's, dream. A straightforward way to have their family sons; daughters; grandchildren; great grandchildren; great, great grandchildren; and their spouses all together here for eternity.

If this is not a shining example of family, then I don't know what is.

TITLE?

In the year 1999, I had worked myself up from four terms on the Board of Directors, to National Treasurer, National Secretary, National Vice President, till at last, I was elected nationwide as National President to the National Association of Independent Fee Appraisers.

My installation was done in the Landmark Hotel in Philadelphia, PA. In addition, I was appointed to be the Convention Chairman. Which was a double privilege ?

I arranged tours in the historic sections of Philly and other tours. I then asked my friend and superstar Al Albert if he could entertain me. Al and his nineteen-piece band gave us a great night. He sang all his award-winning songs and many Italian songs. On this very day, Al's wife had heart problems. He did not leave as I would have, but he was an hour late. He performed as a star, and no one knew he was hurting. Then my friend would not let us pay him. We played the band, but not Al. This was a gift to me, he said.

On the same program, I had the Downtown Mummers perform and they blew the roof off. Few folks had ever seen or heard of them until that day. I hired Ben Franklin and his crew to be dinner speakers. His drum and pipe team played outside the doors as the members arrived for lunch.

The night came and my Julie was the dais as I was sworn in as President.

I was the elected National President of one of the country's largest most respected and poplar real estate appraisal organizations and was personal friends of most of the leaders in the Real Estate and Real Estate Appraisal Industries in the United States and Canada.

I could not help thinking that without the love, the faith, and the sacrifices

Julie made, I would not be this man and have accomplished all that I had. As she kissed me after. Do you think she said, "I'm proud of you," "Congratulations," or anything like that? No—-She said what she always did after each thing I accomplished or any awards that I received. While we danced that night, Julie whispered in my ear simply, "Not bad for a guy with a 7th-grade education."

Yes, it was true that I did the work. But to have this wonderful woman, my wife, lover, friend, and partner guide, push, encourage, and sacrifice for her husband shows an undying love. If she had not, I have no idea of where our life would have taken us. All I know is that because of her love, devotion, confidence, and faith in me, we lived a comfortable, loving, and terribly interesting life.

I was indeed blessed and still am to this day. A notable example is just being able to author this story. To select, spell, and pick the correct words to tell you this entire story. At one time in my life long ago, it would have been considered unthinkable.

No, I have no idea of what my life would have been, if these series of events did not occur in my life. If I had not met Julie once again at Susan's.

So.

This day was now part of my yesterday. The music stopped and we moved on in our lives. Our children were now having their own lives and Julie and I started to enjoy our life, just the two of us again.

The years went by, and I no longer traveled or taught. However, I continued to appraise. Since I turned out to be one of those rare people that actually loved what he does. To this day, at the time of this writing, I work every day.

The years went by and during that time, I had a few heart attacks, totaling four, and three congestive heart attacks, which I never let bother me. And yes, as soon as I could, I was back at work.

Then in 2005, our son David remarried and brought into our lives his new wife Theresa "Terri" Snatiation MacNicoll. Julie and I loved her and her parents on the very first day we met. Then in 2007, Julie and I were blessed with our first grandchildren. David and his wonderful wife Terri gave birth to twins. A boy and girl. They named them Shane and Juliette MacNicoll. Julie was so proud, and she loved them so much.

 This is my life story. Let me end this request from my family to record our family's tale, with these final words:

I know I have repeated it many times in this story, that I love and adore words and their meaning. However, even with my effort here, I fear that I have not really found the right words to explain my love for this woman and just what she meant to me in life. I look forward to being with her again.

Lastly:

My bride Julie would die of cancer to her breast, it took only 44 days and she left me, I was so hurt and completely devastated. It was so hard to think that my bride of 51 years was gone, so I wrote this very last poem that I will never write using the words I felt that last night.

The last night I sat beside you,
Could you feel me there?
My heart was wrapped around you,
As I was stroking your hair.

I was remembering all the good times,
For me they were every single day.
I just wanted you to feel love and comfort,
And happy in some way.

As sat and watched your every breath,

And prayed that each one wasn't your last.
The time we still got to share together,
Went by too quick...Too fast.

I wanted you to wake up,
Please Julie...Please open your eyes.
God, tell me this is just a nightmare,
And not our goodbyes.

As your last breath grew closer,
The family was all here together.
My heart was slowly breaking,
Because I wanted you forever.

Then late at night there it was,
Your final breath of air.
I didn't want to believe it,
This is so cruel and not fair.

As I held your beautiful face,
And prayed that you'd breath again.
I wasn't ready for you to go,
I couldn't admit that this was the end.

Then slowly I realized that you were

now in peace,
And not suffering anymore.
You were beginning the life of an Angel,
And your body would no longer be sore.

I wanted to hold you close and
squeezed you tight,
I didn't want to ever say goodbye.
I've lost my bride, my lover, my number
one best friend,
But I was just helpless all I could
was cry.

I slowly got up,
I wanted so much to stay.
I leaned over and gave you one more
kiss,
It was so hard to walk away.

Julie you were my entire world,
And I miss you so very much.
At night I wish I could feel your loveable
cuddle,
And your soft and gentle touch.

But for now I have to wait,

Until we meet again.
You will always be in my heart and thoughts,
My dear wife, lover and best friend.

The End.

As I told you, her grandfather's maid hated my mother and fold her repeatedly that her family was scum.

Upset her grandfather told her that there was royalty in their family years ago it was even impossible to learn about relatives unless passed on by parents. But years after my mother passed, it was her wish that I research and find our ancestry. I did and she would have been amazed as we her children, grandchild and great grandchildren are. Our ancestry is incredible and unbelievable as you will see.

To prove, I had listening to the parent about each children to prove. Our ancestors are folks that are famous to this world. I hope you read them all down to me.

A list of all my blood great-great-grandfathers and great-great grandmothers.

Relationship to me

Gaius Julius Caesar (100 - 44)
son of Gaius Julius Caesar III the Elder

Cleopatra of Egypt-Wife of Gaius Julius Caesar- My Great-great stepmother

Gaius Julius Caesar I (186 - 166)
son of Gaius Julius Caesar

Julia of Rome (182 - 151)
daughter of Gaius Julius Caesar I

Marcus Atius Balbus (148 - 87)

son of Julia of Rome

Gaius ANTONIUS (142 - 87)

son of Marcus Atius Balbus

Marcus Atius "The Elder" Balbus (148 - 87)

son of Gaius ANTONIUS

Praetor Marcus Atius- The Younger Balbus (105 - 52)

son of Marcus Atius "The Elder" Balbus

ALTA BALBA Caesonia (85 - 43)

daughter of Praetor Marcus Atius- The Younger Balbus

Gaius Rufus (- 58)

son of ALTA BALBA Caesonia

Gaius I OCTAVIUS (200 - 100)
son of Gaius Rufus

GAIUS RUFUS (- 58)
son of Gaius I OCTAVIUS

Gaius Octavius (63 - 59)
son of GAIUS RUFUS

Ancaria MAJOR (156 - 206)
daughter of Gaius Octavius

Gaius Rufus Praetor Rome OCTAVIUS THURINIS (182 - 233)
son of Ancaria MAJOR

Octavia Minor II Rome (69 -)
daughter of Gaius Rufus Praetor Rome OCTAVIUS THURINIS

QUINTUS SERVILIUS, "The Elder", General CAEPIO II (110 - 60)

son of Octavia Minor II Rome

Quintus Servilius Younger Caepio 63 ggf (135 - 90)

son of QUINTUS SERVILIUS, "The Elder", General CAEPIO II

Servilia Major (107 - 42)

daughter of Quintus Servilius Younger Caepio 63 ggf

Quintus Marcius Rex (195 - 118)

son of Servilia Major

Marcia Rex (- 195)

daughter of Quintus Marcius Rex

Lucius Julius Caesar

son of Marcia Rex

Gottfried Julius August Caesar (87 - 44)

son of Lucius Julius Caesar

Gaius Calpurnius (44 -)

son of Gottfried Julius August Caesar

Domitia Calvina (45 - 35)

daughter of Gaius Calpurnius

Marcus Appis Junius SilanusTorquatus (- 54)

son of Domitia Calvina

Junia Calva Milonia Caeceana (- 79)

daughter of Marcus Appis Junius SilanusTorquatus

Caius Cassius Longinus (- 67)

son of Junia Calva Milonia Caeceana

Cassia Longina (- 50)

daughter of Caius Cassius Longinus

Empress Domitia Longina (50 - 126)

daughter of Cassia Longina

Publius Domitius Calvisius Tullus Ruso (Patrician) (75 - 117)

son of Empress Domitia Longina

Domitia Lucilla "Minor" Tranjanus (100 - 158)

daughter of Publius Domitius Calvisius Tullus Ruso (Patrician)

Marcus Aurelius Antonius Augustus Emperor Roman Empire (121 - 180)

son of Domitia Lucilla "Minor"
Tranjanus

**Lucius Aurelius Commodus Antoninus
Calusius II Commodus Emperor of the
Roman Empire (161 - 192)**
son of Marcus Aurelius Antonius
Augustus Emperor Roman Empire

**Flavia Claudia Crispina, Empress of the
Roman Empire (192 - 253)**
daughter of Lucius Aurelius Commodus
Antoninus Calusius II Commodus
Emperor of the Roman Empire

**Flavius Valerius "Chlorus the Pale"
Constantius I Chlorus Emperor of the
West Roman Empire (250 - 306)**
son of Flavia Claudia Crispina, Empress
of the Roman Empire

Constantine I "Constantine the Great" Roman Emperor (287 - 337)

son of Flavius Valerius "Chlorus the Pale" Constantius I Chlorus Emperor of the West Roman Empire

Galla di Roman Empire (315 -)

daughter of Constantine I "Constantine the Great" Roman Emperor

Marina Severa (320 - 373)

daughter of Galla di Roman Empire

Galla Western Roman Empress Roman Empire (347 - 394)

daughter of Marina Severa

Aelia Galla Placida Placidia Empress of Rome (389 - 450)

daughter of Galla Western Roman Empress Roman Empire

Adelphus Adulphus King of the Visigoths (420 - 441)

son of Aelia Galla Placida Placidia Empress of Rome

Eurica of Goths (439 -)

daughter of Adelphus Adulphus King of the Visigoths

Thrasamund King of the Vandals (470 - 523)

son of Eurica of Goths

Amalberga of the Vandels (490 - 540)

daughter of Thrasamund King of the Vandals

Radegonde de Thuringe (510 - 587)

daughter of Amalberga of the Vandels

Oda A Suevian de Souabe (562 - 640)
daughter of Radegonde de Thuringe

Saint Arnoldus Bishop de Metz
Merovingian Heristal (582 - 640)
son of Oda A Suevian de Souabe

Ansegisel "Ansigise" Mayor of the
Palace of Austrasia (606 - 679)
**son of Saint Arnoldus Bishop de Metz
Merovingian Heristal**

Father Pepin II The Fatthe Mediocre
Mayor the Palace DeHeristal (635 - 714)
**son of Ansegisel "Ansigise" Mayor of the
Palace of Austrasia**

Charles - Karl "The Hammer" Martel,
Mayor of the Palace in Austrasia (676 -

741)

son of Father Pepin II The Fatthe
Mediocre Mayor the Palace DeHeristal

Pepin III "The Short" Carolingian King of The Franks (714 - 768)

son of Charles - Karl "The Hammer"
Martel, Mayor of the Palace in Austrasia

Charlemagne Charles "The Great" Carolingian Holy Roman Emperor (742 - 814)

son of Pepin III "The Short" Carolingian
King of The Franks

Louis I Pious KING OF FRANCE France (778 - 840)

son of Charlemagne Charles "The Great"
Carolingian Holy Roman Emperor

Charles II 'the Bald' Karl II of Germany Carolus Holy Roman Emperor King of France (823 - 877)

son of Louis I Pious KING OF FRANCE
France

Roger Comte du MAINE (866 - 900)

son of Charles II 'the Bald' Karl II of Germany Carolus Holy Roman Emperor King of France

Geoffrey Herve Coun du Maine (890 - 942)

son of Roger Comte du MAINE

Aubri III Comte de Gatinais (950 - 1000)

son of Geoffrey Herve Coun du Maine

Geoffroy De Gatinais (953 - 1024)

son of Aubri III Comte de Gatinais

Count of Gastinois Geoffrey II (1004 - 1046)

son of Geoffroy De Gatinais

Ivo Fitzrichard de Roumare deTaillebois (1036 - 1094)

son of Count of Gastinois Geoffrey II

LUCY Countess of Chester TAILLEBOIS (1074 - 1136)

daughter of Ivo Fitzrichard de Roumare deTaillebois

Adeliza Alice De Meschines (1096 - 1136)

daughter of LUCY Countess of Chester TAILLEBOIS

Roger the Good Earl of Hertford deClare* (1116 - 1173)

son of Adeliza Alice De Meschines

Richard III -29 FitzRobert 4th Earl of Hertford "Magna Charta Baron" DeClare (1153 - 1218)

son of Roger the Good Earl of Hertford deClare*

Isabel deClare (1178 - 1213)

daughter of Richard III -29 FitzRobert 4th Earl of Hertford "Magna Charta Baron" DeClare

Edward Le Ryche II (1210 - 1255)

son of Isabel deClare

John Le Riche (1255 - 1307)

son of Edward Le Ryche II

Jean LeRyche (1280 - 1320)
son of John Le Riche

Robert LeRich (1310 - 1353)
son of Jean LeRyche

John LERich (1332 - 1413)
son of Robert LeRich

Richard Rich (1370 - 1415)
son of John LERich

Sir Richard II Rich (1400 - 1464)
son of Richard Rich

Thomas Rich (1432 - 1490)
son of Sir Richard II Rich

Lord Richard Rich (1470 - 1503)
son of Thomas Rich

Lord Richard 1st Baron of Leighs Lord Chancellor of England Rich (1496 - 1567)
son of Lord Richard Rich

Alice Rich (1542 - 1596)
daughter of Lord Richard 1st Baron of Leighs Lord Chancellor of England Rich

Robert White (1560 - 1617)
son of Alice Rich

Elizabeth White (1591 - 1676)
daughter of Robert White

Elizabeth Goodwin (1617 - 1686)
daughter of Elizabeth White

Sarah Crow (1647 - 1719)
daughter of Elizabeth Goodwin

Mary Crow White (1665 - 1750)
daughter of Sarah Crow

Noah Welles Jr (1686 - 1753)
son of Mary Crow White

Noah Welles (1718 - 1776)
son of Noah Welles Jr

Sarah Welles (1752 - 1783)
daughter of Noah Welles

Catherine Livingston (1774 - 1808)
daughter of Sarah Welles

Elizabeth Breese (1797 - 1884)
daughter of Catherine Livingston

Elizabeth Sands (1821 - 1907)
daughter of Elizabeth Breese

Joseph R Cole (1859 - 1942)
son of Elizabeth Sands

William James Cole (1886 - 1950)
son of Joseph R Cole

Emma Mae Cole (1910 - 1989)
daughter of William James Cole

Edwin Patrick MacNicoll Jr. (1936 -)
son of Emma Mae Cole

m

Made in the USA
Middletown, DE
18 October 2023

40856863R00139